THE BOOK OF JAKE

Steve Lerner

The Book of Jake

By Steve Lerner

Hekate Publishing First Edition, 2019

Cover Image by A..F. Knott

ISBN: 978-1-912017-95-9

Hekate Publishing

73 John Drive

Farmingville, NY 11738

admin@hekatepublishing.com

https://www.hekatepublishing.com

ONE

My name is Jake, short for Jacob, who, as you probably know, is a big deal in the Bible. Not as big as Adam or Eve or Noah or Moses, but once you get past the glitz and into the more subtle underpinnings of our hypothetical spiritual origins, you're going to find Jacob pretty interesting. When I was in my teens, I cracked open a Bible. Here's what I learned: Jacob is the prototypical opportunist in the history of the world.

Quick background. In ancient times, the firstborn male inherited everything. Little brothers didn't get crap. Now, it so happened that Jacob had a twin, but firstborn is firstborn, whether by two years and seven months or five minutes and nine seconds. Mom Rebecca goes into labor; the fight is on. Twin Esau sticks his head out, it looks like he's firstborn, he'll never have to work. But wait. As the midwife guides him gently out of Mom, she notices a precious little hand clamped to his ankle trying to pull him back in.

Now, *that's* an opportunist.

Jacob's initial attempt at claiming the inheritance is unsuccessful; all he gets for the effort is a ride into the world on the ankle express, and the name Jacob, which is Hebrew for "heel grabber." Which he probably gets tired of explaining to people when he meets them.

Esau is uncommonly hairy for a newborn, so he is given the name Esau, which means "hairy," a more appealing name than "heel grabber," especially if you stand to inherit land, silver and hundreds of goats.

But Jacob isn't done, not by a longshot. He's a determined boy, and as far as he is concerned the inheritance is still up for grabs. A few years go by. One day Esau walks up to Jacob and says he's hungry, he needs something right away or he's going to faint. Opportunity has knocked. As it happens, Jacob has some food handy and suggests an exchange for the birthright. Esau, his judgment clouded by hunger pangs, says sure, why not. I have never looked into what ancient Talmudic scholars had to say about whether this would have been legally binding or not, but Jacob isn't one to take chances. More years go by. Their father Isaac is dying. His eyesight is fading, so Jacob puts on one of Esau's shirts, robes, whatever, and sticks some goat hair on his arm and visits Dad. Clinging to his last moments of earthly life, Isaac reaches for Jacob's arm, feels the goat hair, thinks it's Esau, gives him the birthright.

I don't remember who ends up inheriting the land, the silver, the goats, what have you, but a few years later, Jacob spends the night wrestling with God. As you would expect, God wins, he's God, but Jacob has proven his tenaciousness, and his name is changed to Israel, which means "perseveres."

As of this moment, I'm still Jake.

Unlike Bible Jacob, I am not a twin. Also, I have

only one wife. Bible Jacob had two. On top of which, he fathered a child with the maid. Which I almost did. Which is how I got to be living at the Cheshire Motel on 6th.

In the Bible, Jacob's wife actually encouraged him to have sex with the maid. She wasn't having any luck getting pregnant and she wanted a baby because she was competing with Jacob's other wife to produce a child and it was *her* maid so she'd be ahead. Not the case with my wife. Vastly different cultures. Anyway, Tess and I were already in consultation with divorce attorneys when I bedded down the maid, and in my opinion when two people agree that a marriage is over, they are no longer married in the biblical sense. Only the paperwork remains. I never cheated on Tess before we said that word, "divorce." But then, yeah.

The Esau in my story is my ex-best friend Roger. His family moved into our neighborhood when we were both five years old. Looking back, I probably should have known that he was a self-centered cocksucker. I did suspect it, but figured, because I was so young, that I lacked sufficient life experience to have opinions of much value, so I ignored the instinctual revulsion. But there was another factor: I was lazy when it came to choosing friends.

I suspect it's normal for a child, upon first venturing into the world, to evaluate members of his peer group and establish bonds with those who meet certain standards and reciprocate interest. Being lazy, my method was this: whoever showed up with any degree of regularity was my friend. To put it another way, whatever mud hit the windshield and stuck would accompany me down the road of childhood.

When I was five, Roger hit the windshield. Splat. He wasn't someone who met any particular standards. We were the same age, he lived nearby; thus: friendship. To carry the mud-hitting-the-windshield metaphor one step further, I should have turned on the wipers.

It's not like he spent his mornings in the backyard torturing cats and setting chaise lounges on fire. However, there *were* occasions when I witnessed him bullying smaller boys. I only remained his friend because I believed these to be passing episodes. After all, he lived in a broken home, his parents having divorced when he was three. His father's visits were brief and sporadic, like those of a largely disinterested cousin. This, I believed, might account for a lot of hostility. But what really distinguished Roger was something else. At the time, I assumed it was a common personality trait, but I have never since met a child who was so completely and irredeemably an egomaniac. Which means he's been able to take it to a higher level than the other, later-blooming egomaniacs. He cheated at sports and games, and defended his brazen tactics with the passion and determination of a high-priced attorney. Yet none of this ever stopped him from sensing a certain rare nobility in himself.

Given this unique set of personality traits, he

headed off to business school. After all these years, I still don't know much about his job except that he wears a suit and spends a lot of time at his desk. Maybe he analyzes reports. I don't know. Not that Roger could analyze anything. What he *could* do is stare at a report for a long time and not get bored, relishing the feeling of looking useful and important. That's how shallow he is.

Why his wife Louise fell for him is a mystery. I'd often notice something deep in her eyes as she'd look at me across the table when the four of us were out to dinner; a sort of "you know him, tell me I'm wrong" look.

My wife Tess has never liked him, and it's probable that the contrast he provided made me more attractive to her. I think I've harbored a subconscious gratitude to him for that all these years.

I'll never say a bad word about Tess. I've often wondered if what she really needs isn't someone exactly like herself but with a penis. We started out well, but at some point our magic carpet turned into a throw rug. I still remember romantic evenings, with the starlit sky shimmering and the ocean purring, the two of us strolling hand in hand along the pier. We'd pause in the moon shadow of some enormous yacht, embrace and kiss, and then cling to one another as if we'd never let go. If life was a moonlit pier, we'd have been fine.

It's not, so now I'm in a motel.

One day I'm lying in bed in my motel room. I'm

fully clothed, watching TV. When you're married, you can't sleep in your shirt and pants, so I'm living it up. I'm watching superhero cartoons, flipping through my mental Rolodex of local drive-thru menus, and it's looking good for the chili cheeseburger but the choice of sides is holding things up. That and I don't feel like moving. I'm doing everything I can think of that would drive Tess crazy. In the back of my mind, I can hear a faint, triumphant shout echoing, as if carried by sacred winds from across the sea. It is the impassioned cry of the Reverend Martin Luther King: "Free at last! Free at last! Free at last!"

The phone rings. It's Roger.

"I just killed a hooker," he says. "What are you doing?"

"Watching *Super Friends*," I say, and hit the mute button on the remote. "What?"

"I just killed a hooker."

"What does *that* cost?" I'm not being flippant, I just don't think he's serious.

Roger sighs.

"You killed a hooker?" I ask.

"It was an accident. I need your help."

I glance at the television. A new cartoon has begun, and the words *Super Friends* blaze across the screen.

"You need my help?"

"Jake..." There is a four-second pause. Roger has a natural sense of timing. "You owe me, buddy."

"Yeah, I owe you. Maybe a stock tip. A ride to

the airport."

He is silent. I can sense him glaring over the phone.

"You want me to help you dump a dead hooker in the river?"

"Will you help me?"

"Fuck, no."

"I'll pay you."

Perhaps I *am* a Super Friend. But I remain silent. He hasn't mentioned a figure yet.

"Jake, I'm screwed," he says.

"Where's Louise?"

"Mount Pleasant, visiting her parents. Come on."

"No way. I'm not helping you dispose of your dead hooker."

"Buddy..." My sense is that he has stopped glaring and is now staring, red-eyed and helpless, into space. "I'm calling in all my chips."

This means I won't owe him any more favors unless he kills another hooker.

"Holy shit, Roger." I sound like I'm weakening. Wisely, he says nothing. "You'll pay me?"

"Yes. Okay?"

I glance at the TV. The Super Friends are meeting in their secret lair and they look worried. "All right, give me a half hour." I don't really need a half hour, but I want that chili cheeseburger, probably a side of onion rings. I hang up.

I get to Roger's house and he looks at me funny. I think he can smell the chili. He leads me upstairs to the bedroom, carrying a bucket of soapy water and a handful of rags. On the floor in the center of the room is a rolled-up carpet concealing something bulky.

"There she is," he says. We stand over the carpet, studying it. "Two things. First, she lost an earring. It might be under the bed, in the bed, in the bathroom, I don't know." He looks pale, haggard, like he needs a nap and two pints of blood. "I'll get the money and make some coffee." He holds out the rags and bucket. "After you find the earring, scrub all the hard surfaces– doorknobs, dressers, bed frame. She was touching everything."

"Mm."

With a conspicuous absence of enthusiasm, I accept the rags and bucket.

"We'll have some coffee," he says, "and come up with a plan."

He leaves before I can say cream, no sugar.

I get down on my hands and knees, crawl around and, after five minutes, finally find the fucking earring between a leg of the bed and the wall. I rest on my haunches and do a quick accounting of all wooden, plastic and metal surfaces where a roving hooker might leave fingerprints, and there's a shit load. Fuck it. I get to my feet and exit the bedroom. We'll hire a housecleaning service after we dump the hooker in the river.

I go to the kitchen, where there's no coffee brewing. I wander through the house calling Roger's name. I check the garage, the backyard.

There have been a lot of schmucks in the history of the world, but I am the current number one. I go back upstairs to the master bedroom and crouch before the rolled-up carpet. I try to peel back the layers at one end but I can't, so I move to the side, take a firm grip of an edge and give it a tug. Louise rotates twice and comes to a stop, eyes aimed upwards, arms splayed out like a grand entrance. She seems surprised to see me, but this was the expression on her face when she realized Roger was murdering her. I must look surprised, too. I was expecting a hooker. We gape at each other.

I jump up and head for the door. I know Roger; he's a good planner. I'll bet the police are on their way and the front door has been left wide open. Then I stop. I turn and walk back to Louise's body, and, metaphorically, I reach up and grab the heel of that son of a bitch.

TWO

I'm lying on my motel bed, still in the shirt and pants I slept in, eating cookies and watching a movie about radioactive mutant crabs the size of liquor stores that attack scientists on a small tropical island. This would kill Tess. The phone rings.

Around ring number seven, I reach lazily for the phone. The handset still inches from my ear, I hear Roger's faint voice, as if calling from the bottom of a deep well.

"Jake? Jake?"

"Just a minute," I say as a mutant crab withstands a hail of gunfire and swings its giant claw perilously close to a lady scientist in a bathing suit. I mute the TV with the remote and pop another cookie into my mouth.

"Roger?" I say.

"Jake? Are you eating?"

I already have a brain buzz from all the sugar, but shove another cookie in and now have to breathe through my nose.

"Uh-huh. Choggud-cubbud mahmel. (Chocolate-covered marshmallow.)

"What?"

"Juh a ih-ih." (Just a minute.) I have a swig of root beer and clear my mouth. "Chocolate-covered marshmallow."

"Mallomars?"

I check the bag. "Yeah."

"What happened?"

I repeat his words, but with a sarcastic, descending pitch. "What happened?" My brain is still preoccupied with the cookies. It's wondering if a little raspberry jelly in the center of the marshmallow might make them even more stimulating. Nothing is ever perfect. And let's face it, even if they did have jelly centers, I'd be thinking about a thicker chocolate shell.

"At the house," says Roger. He's trying to sound in good humor but also a bit baffled.

I decide that if the cookies had raspberry jelly *and* a thicker chocolate shell, they'd be perfect. I reach into the bag for another one anyway.

"With the hooker," prompts Roger.

"Ah, the hooker." Same sarcastic, descending pitch. I drop the latest cookie back into the bag and settle back, nestling into the large motel pillow. "I saw her, Roger."

"Saw who?"

"Louise."

He's thinking, but then realizes I know he's thinking.

"Where is she?" he asks.

"Well, I knew her pretty well; my guess would be Heaven."

He sighs impatience. "The body, Jake."

"What you should have done, Roger, is you should have had some coffee brewing. I go down to the kitchen and nothing, I mean *nothing*, is percolating. This makes me suspicious."

"What the fuck are you talking about?"

"When I figured out that you left, I ran upstairs, to wipe my fingerprints off the bucket, and, just out of curiosity, I unrolled the carpet. After I hopped the fence in the backyard, I went back around the corner and saw a police car pull up at your house."

"A *police* car? Whoa." He pretends to think. "There *have* been a few robberies in the area." He chuckles in a warm, endearing way. "Shit, buddy, somebody must have thought you were a burglar." Roger can go from glaring to ingratiating faster than anybody. "What'd you do with the body?" he asks, just wondering.

"So what's the story? You were out of coffee and ran to the store?"

"No. I..." Lies take time. "I had a few things to do. When I got back, you were gone. Shit, I figured you panicked. So the *police* came. Geez, buddy. What happened?"

"I'll tell you what happened. They went in the house, because you had conveniently left the door wide open."

"That's bullshit!" Glaring again. Amused, glaring, amused, glaring. The idea being I'd rather deal with amused than glaring so I'd stop being a smart-ass.

"You murdered Louise and tried to frame me."

"*What?*" The key to lying is believing yourself. "Hold on. Back up. I told you. It was an accident."

"You said it was a hooker."

"That's right. So that you'd help me. I couldn't tell you it was *Louise*."

"Did you think I'd not notice never seeing her again?"

"I couldn't tell you *then*. I was going to tell you *later*."

"Bullshit. You set it up so that the police would go upstairs, find Louise rolled up in a carpet, and me cleaning fingerprints off the dresser."

"Where do you come up with *that*? I told you, I don't *know* who called the police." He pauses. "Look, Louise and I had a fight..."

"And you accidentally killed her."

"*Yes*." Like I'm being dense.

"What was your alibi? I'm in the bedroom with Louise. Where are you?"

"Jake, we're going in circles."

"All right," I say, "no more circles. I hid the body."

"Where? The attic?" Like it's a guessing game and if he guesses right I have to tell him.

"It's a big house, Roger. And there's the garage, the backyard. Maybe I put her on the roof. You'd find her eventually, but if you're not at Mario's in fifteen minutes with the twenty thousand dollars that we both know is in your safe..."

"Twenty thou…"

"Uh-uh. Stop. You were drunk and you showed me. So shut up. If you say one word– one single fucking word– I will hang up and call the police." I wait for a cruelly long time during which he must remain silent. "If you are not at Mario's with the twenty thousand dollars in exactly fifteen minutes, I will call the police and tell them you confessed to murdering Louise and told me where you hid the body and that you asked me to help you dump her in the river. But, being such a conscientious guy, I decided to turn you in. Some of which is true."

Sixteen and a half minutes later I'm sitting at a sidewalk table at Mario's Bistro speaking into my cell phone.

"Homicide Desk, please."

Roger approaches, holding a briefcase against his stomach. I look up, place a hand over the phone.

"Just a minute," I whisper to Roger, then speak into the phone. "I'll have to call you back." I hang up.

"Sorry I'm late," says Roger.

"Not at all."

Roger sits across the table from me and rests the briefcase in his lap. He tries to glare but the wattage is low.

"Tell me everything," I say, and slide forward in my chair, lean back, and stare up at the sky.

"I was playing golf," he begins.

"Golf will fuck with you."

“Mickey sends me out with these three Japanese guys,” says Roger. “None of them speak English. I say *konichiwa*, they say *konichiwa*, we all laugh, everyone's having a great time. We're trying to chitchat-- you know, nice day, point at the sun, smile. At one point I imitate an airplane..." Roger sticks out his arms sideways and moves them around like an airplane veering left and right, "and I say, 'When you going back to Japan?' They know the word 'Japan' and they can see that I'm an airplane, so when I point to my watch, one of them figures it out and translates for the others. They all point at the ground, which means 'today.' They're leaving today." He leans forward. "And then it hits me. No one knows these guys. Mickey sees me head out with them, come back with them; he's my alibi-- I can prove I was at the golf course till three o'clock. On the sixth tee, I tell them I have to take a crap. I point at my ass." He mimics a splash and the pressing of a lever. "They think that's hilarious. They're doubled over. They can barely breathe. I head to the restroom but cut over to the parking lot and drive home. When I get back, they're on the sixteenth fairway." He turns both palms up: Voila. "We finish the eighteen holes and pass Mickey on the way to the bar. I say *konichiwa*, they say *konichiwa*, Mickey says *konichiwa*, everyone's laughing their heads off. Who could forget that? I buy drinks for everyone and put it on my credit card, which proves I was in the bar after eighteen holes, getting drunk with three Japanese guys who no one knows where the fuck they are."

"They thought you were in the bathroom for nine holes?"

"Yeah." Roger is unfazed; he knows it's a good

story. He watches me, a smug grin on his face like it'll hit me any second how perfect it is. I remain unimpressed, and after a few seconds his mood deteriorates and he is maudlin. "She was leaving me, Jake. She was going to screw me out of everything."

"Uh-huh."

He shakes his head like I don't get it. "She met Daphne."

"Who's Daphne?" I ask the sky.

"Oh, she was..." His head bobs up and down, side to side, as he seeks the correct word.

"A tryst?" I suggest.

He scrunches his nose. "A dalliance."

"Jesus. Who comes up with these words?"

"I know," he says. "I met her at the airport and we fucked."

"Exactly."

"She knew I had money, so she calls Louise and tells her what's been going on and says she feels bad about it and wants to come to the divorce hearing and discuss me with the judge, which will up the settlement and the alimony. Then she tells me about her arrangement with Louise and mentions that she's never had time to travel so now she'd like to see the entire world but she needs a hundred thousand dollars and then she can be out of the country during the hearing."

"You left something out," I say.

"What's that, buddy?"

"The part where I go to prison."

He exhibits signs of a tortured conscience.

"Jake..." He stares into the void, shakes his head. "I regret that. I really do. I was desperate." We both stare into the void. "What can I say? I'm a piece of shit. I know you won't believe this, but I'm glad it worked out this way."

He lifts the briefcase, places it on the table and slides it towards me.

"Here's the twenty thousand," he says.

I stare at the expensive leather briefcase. I think I get it, too.

"There's another ten thousand in the car," he says, "if you help me out of this mess."

"No way, man. That's aiding and abetting..." I say, searching for more legal terminology, "after the fact."

"What do you think you've *been* doing?" he says, and ticks off my aidings and abettings on his fingers. "You didn't call the police; you hid the body; you demanded money..."

"That's not aiding and abetting," I say." That's extortion."

He scoffs. "Same thing. I mean, I'm not a lawyer..."

"No, I think you'rc right."

"We go to the bank," he says, "and deposit the twenty thousand. That's my insurance. You change your mind, I can prove that you blackmailed me. We'll have to trust each other. Then we come up with a plan, make it look like a mugging or something, you get another ten grand."

It's raining money. We go to three banks and I open three small accounts so it won't look like I've just blackmailed someone.

It wasn't so long ago you opened a new account, the bank gave you a toaster, maybe a coffee mug. But things have changed. Today when you open a new account, they give you a high-tech gadget or cash. In new-account gifts, I have now acquired two hundred dollars plus something in a sealed box on the backseat that the new-accounts lady probably mentioned but I didn't catch because I was engrossed in trying to look law-abiding. This day keeps getting better and better. Roger will give me the additional ten thousand dollars tonight, but I know it means more gifts.

We leave my car at Mario's Bistro, and, as Roger drives, I'm daydreaming about the new woman I'll be taking out to an expensive French restaurant and using my new high-tech gadget with. As we pull into Roger's driveway, it occurs to me that, once inside the house, Roger could crack me on the head with the bronze sculpture on the glass table by the front door and his problems won't be significantly worse than they are now. He shuts off the engine and opens his door.

"Let's go," he says, because I haven't moved.

He has one foot on the pavement and he's waiting. I am preoccupied with visions of the brass sculpture crashing into my skull, me crumpling to the ground, and Roger rolling me up in a carpet. I'm thinking: he's already killed once; *that's* the tough one. I'm waiting for someone to come strolling along, maybe walking their dog, so I can introduce myself, first and last name, date of birth, and have a memorable conversation. Roger would have second thoughts about killing me if there was a witness who saw me in front of his house two minutes before my official time of death. I scan the neighborhood but it's a ghost town. I step out of the car, staying on the balls of my feet, ready to maneuver. I decide to keep some distance between us, and, if he tries to kill me, to demand more money.

We enter the house and Roger closes the door.

"Where is she?" he asks.

I place myself strategically between Roger and the bronze sculpture.

"Where's your gun?" I ask.

"What?"

"Your gun."

He exhibits puzzlement.

"Roger, be honest, you'd be better off if I was dead."

"*Jesus*, Jake..." He looks stunned. His body slumps in disbelief.

"You tried to frame me for murder. I would have gone to prison."

"Yes, *prison*," he says. "I wouldn't *kill* you." He is astonished at my poor reasoning.

"You killed Louise."

He straightens, thinks about it, sees my point.

"All right," he says, and turns and heads upstairs.

I follow him to the master bedroom, where he gestures to a dresser drawer. I open it and, beneath a pair of green pajamas, find the gun. I check the barrel. It's loaded.

"Downstairs," I say.

I direct Roger to the closet in the hallway by the kitchen. Stored inside are various items for parties and special occasions: place mats, cloth napkins, silverware, candleholders. On the floor, beneath a frilly white tablecloth, is the hostess herself.

I lift a corner of the tablecloth, revealing Louise's face. Roger stares, eyes glazed. After a few moments, he wanders away as if in a trance. I get down on my knees and, after a few bangs and bumps, have Louise cradled gently in my arms. She still looks surprised, and who can blame her.

We go in search of Roger and find him sitting in the big easy chair in the shadows of the den.

"What have I done?" he asks, an odd question, considering the woman he just murdered has just been carried into the room by the man he tried to frame. But he means morally.

He looks at Louise. "Why were you so greedy?"

Louise says nothing.

"It's that fucking Daphne," says Roger. "If she doesn't tell Louise about her and me, none of this would have happened."

My back is tired. I set Louise down on the couch and have a seat next to her, wrapping an arm around her shoulders to hold her up. In the reflection of the TV screen, I can see the surprised look on her face. We could be watching a horror movie.

Roger stands. "I'll get a bed sheet," he says, and leaves the room.

Louise and I sit quietly. I am reminded of a blind date I went on in high school when the girl and I struggled to carry on a conversation.

I should call the police. Roger should be held accountable. I hate a man who was my friend since childhood. I feel cold. As cold as Louise.

THREE

It is early evening. Roger and I sit at the kitchen table. Even given what has happened, I did not expect the bond we had shared for all these years to vanish so completely. But it has. We will never again be those two backslapping pals, throwing back beers, reliving childhood adventures. Instead, we may soon be two backstabbing defendants, sipping stale coffee and hashing out plea bargains with our respective attorneys. I do not miss him as a friend. My vague sense through the years that he was a remote and uncaring bastard had apparently been spot-on.

Louise rests quietly in the trunk of her Cadillac. I can remember the day they purchased this Cadillac and how pleased she was with the ample trunk space. This is now a bittersweet memory.

Roger is a fan of classic TV detective shows and knows that Louise's time of death, or TOD, will place him at the golf course. I am a fan of some of the newer ones and know that Roger may soon be in jail and me in South America. We have been tossing ideas around for a half hour. The phone rings.

We stare at the answering machine. Louise's recorded voice is about to speak.

"I can't get to the phone right now," it says with sudden poignancy. I look at Roger. He shrugs. "If you're trying to reach Roger," continues the recording, "please try his cell phone as he no longer lives here and I sure as fuck won't be passing along his messages." Beep.

"I'll erase that," says Roger.

"Oh, sweetie," says Sylvia, "you must be an absolute wreck. I'm calling to apologize about this morning. I took Adelaide to dance and completely forgot about going jogging. Can we go tomorrow? Roger is a bastard. Call me." Beep.

We spend a few moments taking this in. Then Roger stands and goes to the answering machine.

"Louise told you to move out?" I ask.

He frowns. "When I came back from the golf course she was shouting all kinds of shit. I wasn't paying attention."

He presses a button on the answering machine, but it's the wrong one, and again we hear Louise: "I can't get to the phone right now." Fittingly, these will be her last words.

Roger presses more buttons.

"I'll be out for a few hours," he says.

"Where are you going?" I ask.

He presses another button and glares at me.

"I'm recording," he says, and starts over. "I'll be out for a few hours. Louise, if that's you, please call my cell. I'm worried." With this new message recorded, he turns and looks at me, and freezes. He can see I'm onto something.

"Did you erase Sylvia's message?" I ask.

"No."

"Good. Leave it."

He sits down across the table from me and watches me think.

"Did Louise have a place she usually went jogging?" I ask.

"Yeah," says Roger, "a trail in the foothills."

"All right, listen. You get home around five o'clock. Louise isn't here. You play Sylvia's message and you're perplexed: where's Louise? You call Sylvia." Roger listens breathlessly. "It gets late and a burgeoning sense of panic begins gnawing at your gut. You call some of Louise's friends. They're no help. Finally you call the police. In the morning Louise's body is found behind a rock by the jogging trail. Her wallet's there but the money and credit cards are gone."

"No," says Roger. "She'd leave her wallet in the car."

He's right. I think it through, but I can't come up with a reason she'd have her wallet while she's jogging. Screw it.

"Well, she has it. We dress Louise in her jogging clothes, take her to the trail, and stage the scene."

Roger waits for instructions like a dog drooling before a forbidden biscuit.

"Call Sylvia," I say.

He jumps up, goes to the phone, flips through the address book, finds Sylvia's number and dials. Sylvia answers.

"Sylvia!" he says, sounding delighted.

"No!" I whisper. "You're *worried*. She called you a

bastard."

He is grim.

"Sylvia..." he says, but she has interrupted. He shifts into a tone of edgy sarcasm. "What do I *want*? Well, I'm *worried*, Sylvia. Louise isn't here, and I haven't heard from her all day."

He checks in with me and I nod. He smiles. If he had a tail, it would be whipping side to side. He resumes grim and listens to Sylvia.

"I just *said* that," says Roger. "She's not here."

He checks in with me again, but he's checking in too much, so I do nothing.

"I don't know, Sylvia," he says, a subtle tone of dread seeping into his voice. Well done. He listens. "Yes, Sylvia. Yes, we had an argument, and this morning we agreed to have a serious talk about it tonight. Now I get home and there's no note, nothing. If I don't hear from her in..." he looks at his wrist where there is no watch, "half an hour, I'm calling the police." He listens. "Oh, really. Well, fuck you, Sylvia. Oh, my God…" His voice cracks. "Where is she?" He hangs up.

I raise my fists in triumph. Roger is overwhelmed. He may be urinating.

"All right, go get her jogging clothes," I say.

He sprints from the kitchen and up the stairs.

FOUR

It is midnight. Except for being dead, Louise is all set to go jogging. She is wearing a powder-blue jogging suit, zipped to the neck for cold morning weather. For the time being, she relaxes in the trunk. Roger will escort her to the foothills in her car; I will follow in his.

I drive to the end of the block, observe no activity, and call Roger on his cell.

“All clear," I say.

"Roger,” he answers.

I don’t know if he’s saying his name or speaking radio language, but his electric garage door opens, so I hang up.

I lead the way, and Roger follows a half block behind. If anyone should happen to appear before we’re out of the neighborhood, I will cause a distraction while he skulks back to the house. No one must see Roger driving Louise’s car or we’ll need a new plan, and I’m sick of talking to him. All is quiet.

Once on the freeway, I let Roger pass, then follow fifty yards behind and, cleverly, in a different lane. The quiet and solitude allow for some good thinking. I dial Roger.

"Yeah, buddy," he says, just a guy out for a drive.

"How much life insurance did Louise have?"

The long pause signifies he is devastated by my insinuation.

"It had nothing to do with insurance, Jake."

I remain silent but at the same time say so much.

"I'll give it to charity, okay?" he says.

"And something else. In the frame-up, where I supposedly murdered Louise, I'm just curious, what's the story?"

"You were having an affair."

"Me and Louise."

"Yes."

"I see. So she tried to end the affair, but I had become so obsessed that I lost control, grabbed her throat, and tried to shake some sense into her. But, having lost my mind, my sense of time was so impaired that I didn't realize it had been four or five minutes since she'd had a good solid breath and I didn't mean to kill her?"

"Exactly," he says. "It was an accident. You do five, maybe ten years. I tell the police that she confessed about the affair and promised to end it." He pauses. "And I'll tell you something, buddy. She *would* have had an affair with you."

"Excuse me?"

"Shit, you should have heard her." He imitates Louise in an unflattering way. "'Isn't Jake *great*? Why can't *you* be more like him?'" He scoffs. "Everyone has always fucking loved you. Why do you think I've always hated your guts?"

This is the only conversation of any depth we've ever had.

"You've always hated my guts?" I say.

"Yep."

“Even when we were kids?"

"Oh, yes,” he says, reminiscing. “Absolutely. Teachers loved you. My mom was crazy about you. Shit, Jake, my dad never played catch with me unless you were there. Think about that. And be honest, you’ve never liked me, either."

"Now, wait. I’ve never *respected* you," I say. "You’re a self-absorbed asshole, but..." I‘ve said ‘but’ so I have to continue, "I did like you. A little. Sometimes." I pause. "Maybe ‘liked’ is the wrong word."

"See?"

"I just always felt we were *supposed* to be friends."

"Exactly.” He thinks about it. “I’ve always hated you, buddy. But I respected you."

"So you murder Louise and frame me?"

Silence. He is either brooding or sulking. When he next speaks, it is at low volume.

"I was desperate, Jake."

I’ve had enough. "Did you bring the other ten thousand?" I ask.

"It’s in the trunk."

I hang up. We drive in silence. The foothills on my right seem devoid of life; night-shrouded heaps of barren earth. I ask myself: Is it too late to turn back?

No, it is not.

We exit the freeway and travel along the dark road as it winds past an all-night supermarket and a mini mall and upwards into the foothills. My mind wanders back in time. I am seven years old, lying on the front lawn at Roger's house, clutching an imaginary futuristic laser gun. Roger struggles in futility at the base of an olive tree whose exposed, tangled roots are the human brains it has consumed in its quest to acquire power over the Earth and its inhabitants. Roger had rescued me when it was my brain at risk of being ripped out and eaten by the savage tree, so I gather my courage, rise to my feet, and fire round after round of futuristic laser ray beams into the tree's brain amalgamate. Exhausted and injured, Roger crawls to safety.

It's hard to forget something like that.

Roger was the friend with whom I navigated the wonderful and treacherous world of childhood. And now he has betrayed me. So screw it, I'll take the thirty grand and walk away the winner. He can stew in his greed; in the memory of his evil act. Good riddance.

I have only minutes to choose which path I will take. I am at the crossroads of life. I turn left.

I follow Roger's car onto a dirt parking area where the jogging trail begins. This is the crucial moment. Louise's body will be found nearby in the morning, so we must not be seen here. As I step out of the car, Roger approaches. He holds a bulky envelope.

"Here's the ten thousand," he says.

I take the envelope, open the flap, and look inside just to be rude. We go to the trunk of the Cadillac. Roger opens it, and again we see Louise's surprised face. For the first time, I can see the irony. During her final years, Louise had become a woman who was rarely surprised by anything; she had seen it all. She had acquired a jaded exterior; her emotional range had shrunk to a narrow bandwidth of sour tolerance. That's how it seemed, anyway. Maybe cynics want desperately to believe they've seen it all because it allows them the comforting assumption that nothing worse lies ahead.

I take hold of her ankles. Roger grasps her arms. We lift Louise out of the trunk and carry her to where the jogging trail begins. A subconscious sense of place, coupled with a conscious one of urgency, compels us, without a single spoken word, to start jogging. At first it is awkward, Louise hanging between us, jouncing roughly, but after a while we settle into a comfortable trot. Roger and I have always worked well together; like the time, as ten-year-olds, we cleared a half acre of brush from a hill behind a house and the man who was paying us the exploitive wage of a dollar an hour stared at us in wide-eyed amazement when we finished before noon what he probably figured would take the whole weekend. Neither of us has ever tried to be the boss. We were like two superheroes, combining our unique and distinct powers to foil evil, or to make money.

I haven't been jogging in years—I prefer the exercycle in front of my TV—but the crisp night air invigorates, and I'm hoping we can get in a couple of miles before we find a suitable place to leave Louise.

"Stop," whispers Roger.

Like the well-coordinated team we have been since our friendship began, Roger and I come to an abrupt halt. Louise, however, swings sharply forward and is nearly launched.

"What?" I ask.

"Shh."

We try to suppress our loud panting, but the effort results in loud wheezing.

"Did you hear that?" asks Roger. "It sounded like a car door." He looks at me. His eyes are off-kilter and buggy. "What kind of an idiot goes jogging at this time of night?"

Louise and I look at each other but say nothing.

All is quiet.

"Hey," says Roger. "What about there?" He is looking at a Louise-sized space behind a boulder near the rock wall.

And something happens. This is Louise we're talking about. Louise, who thought I was a great guy; Louise, who wished Roger could be more like me; Louise, who, according to Roger, yearned in secret for a small slice of heaven within my embrace. I mean, dear God, what a woman. Not to belabor the point, but a woman who clearly adored me. And now I'm supposed to leave her out here, alone in the chill of night, with the ferrets and the possums and the rats and whatever else might come sniffing around, leave her here, hidden behind a rock like a piece of garbage?

I look at Louise, and silently ask: Why Roger? What could you have seen in him? What psychological flaw drew you to this– how shall I put it– walking rectum? Were you so desperately anxious to be married that you projected onto him the qualities of the kind of man you'd always imagined marrying?

What I think happens is that many women get married with their fingers crossed. They may even suspect that the groom-to-be is not exactly who or what they think, but they don't look too closely because they're happy; they want to believe that their doubts are foolish and unwarranted. So they keep smiling for a few years, gradually become more and more disillusioned, and eventually get murdered. I think of how Louise had changed over the years, but now with new understanding. She had gotten tired of deluding herself, had braced herself for a life that could never be enough for someone with the capacity for love that she possessed. Then Daphne, the mistress, comes along, and even that is impossible.

I will speak for you, Louise.

It's true, Roger will get away with murder, but that is all I can bear. I refuse to profit from it. I will donate the thirty thousand dollars to a charity in Louise's name.

I stand among the dark, barren hills, overcome with disappointment in myself. To this point in my life, I have been only a selfish, hedonistic child. It stops now.

What happens to Roger is not my concern. Maybe he'll meet with divine justice, or bad karma, or maybe we're all just a bunch of statistics and life is a roll of the dice and the dice don't care if you murdered your wife. I don't know.

"We leave her in the car," I say.

Roger sets his half of Louise down. "What?"

"We leave her in the car. That's where she's mugged and that's where she's found."

"Why the fuck didn't you say that before?" he asks.

I guess a little physical activity in the fresh night air clears a mind. I don't say that.

He grumbles, reaches down, and lifts Louise. The part of his psyche which, at birth, might have developed into a conscience must have stirred briefly, like someone gasping softly and smacking their lips before settling back into a deep, restful sleep. On the return trip to the parking area, we move at a leisurely pace, Louise swaying gently between us. It is a long walk, but I don't mind. I've done a good thing.

FIVE

I feel calm; perhaps a byproduct of brand-new scruples. Roger, however, looks nervous. He is no longer talking or blinking. He uses a moist hand towel to clean the steering wheel, door handles, et cetera, of fingerprints. I remove the credit cards and money from Louise's wallet, and we put her in the driver's seat, slumped over, out of sight.

When we have finished, I get behind the wheel of Roger's car and guide us onto the freeway. Roger stares through the windshield at the dark horizon.

"Roger," I say. It's time to review our plan, but I also want to see if he's conscious.

He turns his head slowly and looks at me. He is like a hypnotist's subject, responding to my voice but oblivious to all else.

"When we get back to the house," I say, "we check your answering machine for messages, then you call the police. If anyone asks where you've been for the last hour, tell them you were worried so you went for a drive hoping to spot Louise's car, and that while you were driving you realized how much you loved her, so you promised God there wouldn't be any more dalliances if you got a second chance." Roger is staring into the night with glazed eyes. "Remember to act stressed," I remind him.

As we exit the freeway, I glance over and notice a change. The tension has drained from Roger's body.

He looks crumpled, like a partially deflated basketball.

"Jake," he says, "I'm sorry. Those things I said before…" he turns to face me, his attempt at a sheepish grin ghoulishly misshaping his bloodshot eyes. "I didn't *always* hate you." He shrugs, wrinkles his nose. "Most of the time, but not always."

I hope he's not expecting a hug. "Thanks," I say.

"My marriage," he says, his voice like a child's now, "was constant war. You know?"

I want back all the hours I've spent with him. Those are hours I might have spent napping, or reading great literature, or doing sit-ups. What a waste. I press the accelerator. I want this over with.

On the desk in Roger's kitchen, a little red "3" pulses in the window of the answering machine. Roger gets us a couple of beers from the refrigerator, then presses "play."

As expected, the messages are from Louise's friends. Barb and Linda offer assurances that Louise will show up soon. Sylvia says that Roger is a bastard.

It's time to call the police. Then I can go back to the motel, put on a suit, and go to bed.

Roger goes to the phone, presses the speaker button and dials. As our eyes meet, a tacit agreement is made: I am the director, he is the actor. I hold his attention with unobtrusive yet godlike authority, raise one hand in the air— this means "And..."— then move it slightly– this means "...action." As if he has trained at the Actors Studio, his face and body immediately portray inconsolable anguish. His clothes seem to further rumple. He is in character. While the line rings, he clutches the beer can; the creaking of it jolts him, as if he had forgotten it was there. He is a jumble of dwindling hopes and mounting fears. A woman answers.

"Missing Persons Unit. Detective Torres."

"Good evening, Detective," says Roger amiably. He has failed.

I want to shout "Cut!" but instead raise my hands in a what-the-hell gesture. He adjusts and is immediately transformed: turmoil, anguish, dread.

"My wife..." he says, panting softly. "Something's happened. I haven't heard from her all day. I called her friends." His voice pinched by stress, grows louder. "No one knows where she is. Oh, God..."

He sounds like a man who has just murdered someone. I gesture for him to calm himself, but just a little, like a conductor quieting his orchestra.

"What is your name and address, sir?" asks Detective Torres.

"I'm Roger Kaplan. 10475 Vista Drive." He is calmer, but still exhibits credible undertones of stress.

"And your wife's name?"

"Louise." His voice cracks. Masterful.

"When is the last time you saw or spoke to her?"

He looks at me. I look at him. I can't play the instruments, too. I hold one hand out, palm up, and shake my head. This means: answer the fucking question.

"About six a.m.," he says. "She was still sleeping.

She was supposed to go jogging with Sylvia but Sylvia forgot and she doesn't know if Louise went alone or not. Oh, God."

"Did Louise have any other plans or appointments today?" asks Detective Torres.

Roger checks in with me. I hunch my shoulders and spread my hands, indicating uncertainty.

"I don't know," says Roger.

"Is her car still at your residence?"

Roger looks at me, then realizes he knows that one.

"No."

"All right. Now, if she did go jogging, do you know where that would have been?"

I do the hunched-shoulders-spread-hands thing.

"I don't know," says Roger.

"After we're done talking, I want you to call Sylvia and ask about that."

Roger frowns. Sylvia keeps calling him a bastard.

I raise my eyebrows, indicating directorial impatience.

"Fine, fine," he says.

"Mr. Kaplan, is there any reason why Louise might be upset?" asks Detective Torres. "Why she might want to be by herself?"

Somehow I don't laugh.

"Nope," says Roger, shaking his head. "Nope."

"I see. Is Louise being treated for any medical or psychiatric conditions?"

"No."

"And you said no one you've spoken to has seen or heard from her today?"

"That's right. I went to play golf early and then treated the guys to lunch and drinks at the restaurant. I wasn't home till five."

There is a gentle bumping sound. It is my forehead hitting the table. The schmuck is providing an alibi. Leaving my head on the table, I raise a hand in the air and make several slashing motions. Roger stops talking.

"All right, Mr. Kaplan," says the detective, "I'll need you to stay by the phone in case Louise calls."

This detective is good. She moves right along but has probably just referred the case to Homicide.

"Also," she says, "I need you to get me Louise's credit card numbers, ATM information, cell phone number, and the make, model and license plate of her car. Can you do that?"

"Yes," says Roger.

"Good. And don't forget to call Sylvia about the jogging location. Again, I'm Detective Torres and I'll be here for a couple of hours. If I'm not in when you call, just leave the information with whoever answers. It's good that you called, Mr. Kaplan, but I want to assure you that most of these situations turn out to be a lot of worrying about nothing."

"Oh, God, I hope so," says Roger. "This isn't like her. She *always* calls."

"All right, Mr. Kap..."

"What if she's been in an accident..."

"It doesn't help to go jumping to conclusions, Mr. Kaplan. Just stay calm. I'll need your help..."

"Goddamn it," shouts Roger, "I can't just sit here!"

Ironically, as my hatred for Roger grows, so, too, must my sympathy. This is what it feels like to want to kill someone.

"Mr. Kaplan, please stay calm. Is there anyone who can come over and stay with you?"

Roger's on his own. Screw this.

"Well..." he begins.

"Call me when you have the information I asked for. Good-bye, Mr. Kaplan."

Roger hangs up and looks at me.

"We're fucked," I say.

SIX

The Bible is metaphor. Or is it allegory? I forget the difference. Jacob wrestles with God. He doesn't win, but what happens is, he changes. He goes from being an opportunistic louse who lies and schemes to being a man of principle and purpose. I've done the first part. Now I'm wrestling with the circumstances I've brought upon myself. Whatever happens, whatever trials await me, I must never quit. I must persevere. The Esau of my story is Roger, who is no saint himself. Roger will struggle for a lot of things, but none of them are his soul.

Now, I'm not comparing myself to Bible Jacob. But because the Bible, like most ancient stories, deals with universal themes, people of any historical era, any culture, might draw meaning from it. For example, many people identify with the Bible's David as they are confronted by a Goliath in the form of intimidating circumstances. That's me sometimes. Some identify with Noah as they struggle to keep their lonely ship of righteousness and integrity afloat amidst a deluge of deceit and corruption. I'll call that a goal. Others identify with Adam and Eve, who sin, then lie and equivocate to avoid punishment, but who must ultimately be held accountable for their actions and seek redemption. I identify most closely with Jacob, the opportunistic heel-grabber who wrestled with God and, if nothing else, showed perseverance.

A struggle may be unwinnable yet still make us stronger; stronger for the battles yet to come.

After the phone call to Detective Torres, I go back to the motel. My home is a motel. My marriage is over. My oldest friendship lies in ruins. I've aided and abetted a murderer. I stand in the bathroom and take a long look in the mirror. I think I'm gaining weight.

I sit on the bed.

It is a strange moment, because I am just sitting, not doing anything. Normally, I'd be following the latest urge, the latest appetite, seeking the next stimulation, the next indulgence– cheeseburger and fries, TV, nap, liquor, sex. But I just sit there like those guys in the psychiatric hospital. When I was in college, I worked for a pharmacy delivering medicine to retirement homes and hospitals. One of them was a residence for the mentally ill. As I'd make my way to the nurses' station, listening to the blurted chatter and gibberish of the delusional, I'd see these docile men sitting quietly in the hallways. They had no need of further stimulation. They just sat there and found life interesting.

After what I've been through, I'm up for a few hours of that. It is peaceful but, in a strange way, exciting, too. It is as if I have arrived in a new, exotic, yet oddly familiar city. This is the place of second chances.

SEVEN

It is early Sunday afternoon, and the sense is undeniable: I am becoming a better man. Which, let's face it, is not saying much. I called Tess this morning to see if she'd notice the change. She didn't. She kept saying, "What do you *want?*" You don't know Tess, but she has to push me away like that because she has moved on in life and is on a schedule. She really does love me.

One of my old vices was indulging in meals of absurd dimensions. Imagine an assortment of food laid out in such a way as to imply the involvement of a caterer and an imminent gathering of friends and family. And just me. Such behavior, sometimes referred to as gluttony, must now be curtailed. Still, I did want to celebrate my recent enlightenment, so for breakfast I had pancakes and sausage in boysenberry syrup with hash brown potatoes and a cheese omelet. However afterwards, instead of watching TV until I fell asleep, I went for a brisk walk to the bookstore. I bought a suspense thriller, but also *David Copperfield.* I plan a relaxing evening. New phases of life should be eased into. Or is it plunged into? One can always plunge; easing should be attempted first.

I will start my new diet with a low-calorie, high protein lunch– maybe baked fish with steamed vegetables. As I'm on my way out the door, my cell phone rings. The little screen on the phone says:

Roger. I let it ring. It will be nice to listen to his message as I drive to the restaurant and then delete him. I arrive at Roberta's House of Crabs and access my voice mail.

"Jake," says Roger's voice, "I'm calling about that thing." I'm assuming the murder. "There's been a development." His tone turns cheerful. "Haven't seen you in a while, buddy." He's taking precautions in case the police hear this message after Louise's body is discovered. "Give me a call."

I return to the motel with the baked fish and steamed vegetables. While I eat, I watch half a John Wayne movie and renew my hatred for Nazis, traitors and cowards. I plan a night out at the sports bar with the flirty waitresses and the drunk guys reminiscing about Mookie Wilson and explaining why the Jets will win the Super Bowl and mentioning that their dad moved out when they were eight years old but they still have a good relationship, and somehow, miraculously, never once going to urinate during the three hours I'm there.

I do not want to call Roger. I've just eaten baked fish and steamed vegetables, for God's sake; I'm smack dab in the middle of a new phase of life and Roger's not in it. I don't care about the development with the thing. But then I realize that Roger and I need to have one last conversation. I must make it clear that he is never to contact me again, that he must deal with all future thing developments on his own.

I dial. He answers on the first ring.

"Hey, buddy."

"Never call me again."

"Something happened."

"What?"

"Imagine the worst thing possible."

"You calling me and making me guess why."

"We have to meet."

"Or that."

"I'm serious, buddy."

"You're a shithole. Mario's. Same table." I hang up.

We are sitting at the same sidewalk table as yesterday. I have not said a word; not a hello, not a what's-this-all-about. I am there to listen then leave.

"Someone knows everything," says Roger.

"Who?"

"Remember Daphne?"

"The dalliance?"

"Yeah." He looks around furtively. "She was there."

"Where?"

"In the house." He looks around again to make sure no one is near. "When I..." he widens his eyes and contorts his face in a manner that obliquely references the murdering of his wife.

I speak condescendingly, as to a timid child. "Did you kill her, too?"

"Of course not. Listen. Daphne and Louise struck up a weird relationship based on screwing me at the divorce hearing and Daphne started coming over four, five times a week. They're watching soap operas, game shows, and Daphne's laying this shit on Louise about how she can't make the rent, she needs money for groceries, blah, blah, blah, and Louise is so fucking gullible she's writing checks, two hundred bucks at a time, because Daphne's gonna tell the judge what a lying, philandering asshole I am. So, anyway, she was there that day when I..." He does the face again.

"All right," I say, "I need to ask you a few questions."

Roger stares down at the table and nods, like he knew this was coming.

"Does Daphne have any proof?"

"Yes."

"What?"

"Pictures."

"Pictures."

"Yeah. She took them with her cell phone," he says, disgusted with technology. "There's a couple of me holding a pillow over Louise's face."

"That's incriminating."

"Look." Roger takes his cell phone out, presses some keys and holds the screen up for me to look at. There are a series of photographs: Roger pushing a frilly pillow into Louise's face; still pushing; still pushing; Roger standing over Louise watching her rib cage for signs of breathing.

He closes the cell phone and puts it in his

pocket.

"Does Daphne know about me?" I ask. This is really the only question. The others are decoys.

"No. She said her boyfriend is in on this and if anything happens to her, he'll skull-fuck me. They want two hundred thousand dollars, but they know the police will be watching for a while so they'll take a twenty thousand dollar good-faith payment. I hate to ask you this, buddy, but Daphne knew about the money in the safe and if they don't get the twenty thousand today, they'll send the pictures to the police.

"How did she know about the safe?"

"I got drunk and showed her."

"Fine," I say. "I'll get you the twenty thousand. Fuck it. But then I'm done."

"There's one more thing."

"What?"

"I was thinking about it. After Daphne and her boyfriend spend the two hundred thousand, they could keep coming back for more, and when I stop paying, they'll send the pictures to the police anyway."

"So you're fucked. Tough shit."

"No, Jake. If the police get *me*, they'll know I had help. How else could I get home after I leave Louise in the car?"

The asshole is right. I'm trying to change my life, become a better man, forge a brighter tomorrow, all that crap, and now God wants to wrestle. He has me in a reverse Kimura and is maneuvering for a guillotine choke.

“I’m meeting Daphne tonight to give her the twenty thousand,” says Roger. “After she leaves, you follow her. Find out who the boyfriend is and where he lives.”

“Why?”

“So I can tell Daphne I know who her boyfriend is and that if she sends those pictures to the police, the last thing I’ll do before I go to prison is hire some guys I know that will beat the living shit out of him.”

“You know people like that?”

“Yep.

“All right, listen carefully, Roger. If I get you the boyfriend’s name and the two of them wind up dead, I *will* go to the police.”

“I’m not gonna *murder* them,” says Roger. “I’ll just scare them so they don’t come back asking for more.”

“All right,” I say. “But that’s it. Then I’m gone.”

I hammer-fist God beneath his left ear. He is momentarily dazed, and I scuttle out from underneath, sending a backwards heel kick to his jaw. I am on my feet. But he looks pissed.

EIGHT

It is nine p.m., a beautiful evening. I'm sitting in my car at a corner of Woodley Park. The park is well lit and I'm watching a basketball game a half block away. There is a spherical man, maybe five foot eight, holding a basketball above his head while a couple of short, skinny guys try to slap it loose. The spherical man throws elbows and the little guys scatter. Leading with his monumental paunch, he steamrolls one of them before dishing the ball to a teammate in the corner who shoots and misses. The spherical man grabs the board, dribbles once, fakes left, then, crouching to maximize the inertia of his bulk, bursts upwards through the slashing arms of the defenders to score off the backboard. He has committed six fouls. His opponents lie on the ground panting. Time out is called.

There is a duck pond in the distance. A young couple strolls along its edge. I hear the clop of struck tennis balls in the distance, the occasional rattling slap of ball hitting fence. I find it all very calming. Roger is meeting Daphne here to give her the twenty thousand dollars, and then I will follow her to the boyfriend.

Roger is sitting on a bench next to a drinking fountain by the basketball courts and looks like he's waiting for his blackmailer. He leans forward, elbows resting on knees, and stares at the ground. Who goes to the park to do that?

A blonde woman in a pink jogging suit trots by, ignoring him. She stops at the drinking fountain, turns the spigot, and pretends to drink. I can tell this from a half block away. She straightens, pretends to wipe water from her lips, then turns to face Roger. She is small but imposing, and seems to loom over him like a small swarm of locusts. Neither speaks. When I was a kid, my family had two dogs and a cat. Sometimes at bedtime, as the dogs lay drowsily in their little beds, the cat would enter the room and sit directly in front of one of them and stare for as long as it took until the dog in the contested bed abandoned it and wandered off to find someplace else to sleep. This woman is like that cat. Timidly, Roger stands, then goes in search of someplace else to mope. He has left the envelope containing the money on the bench. The woman sits next to the envelope as if unaware of its presence. She scans the area, arms spread majestically across the bench's back. Satisfied that she is not being observed, she picks up the envelope and gives it a squeeze as if she can count money that way. After a short period of fake rest she stands, briefly stretches her hamstrings, and trots away.

So this is Daphne: temptress, extortionist, jogger.

She crosses the infield of the baseball diamond. There is a parking lot behind the stands, and I drive over in a hurry.

When I arrive, Daphne is at the window of a vending truck, studying the large painted menu above.

She places her order, which is rather extensive, and has the woman inside the truck shouting orders over her shoulder. I wonder if Daphne will pay with a hundred dollar bill from the big envelope, but instead she digs into the pocket of her sweat pants for some crumpled bills. Three minutes later, she is called back to the window and given a bag. She has ordered to go. I am hungry, and if I get the chance I'm going to take the bag.

As she walks past my car, I slouch. When you're a kid, your parents tell you, "Don't slouch. Sit up straight." In spy school– the CIA, Interpol– they probably tell their trainees, "Slouch. No, lower." Children should tell their parents they want to be spies when they grow up so mind your own business.

Daphne gets in her car, a beat-up, once-gold two-door, and starts the engine. She makes a right onto Victory. I count to five, then follow. Now I'm not slouching. That would be too conspicuous. I'm sitting up straight. You really need both.

We drive to a supermarket, and I get out of my car and follow her in. She heads for the back, but I linger midway down a frozen food aisle. The pictures on the boxes of frozen food are enticing. Veal Parmesan with pasta, boneless barbecued ribs and sweet corn, deep-fried chicken tenders with mashed potatoes. There are tantalizing desserts: triple-layer chocolate cake; apple cinnamon tarts. I pause before a box of cherry blintzes, which are both low-calorie and delicious, and could be eaten frozen.

I have lost her. I speed-walk to the row of checkout stands, and there she is, two six-packs of beer cradled in her arms, waiting behind a woman who is preparing for the Armageddon. This woman is alarmingly overweight and will not be able to outrun the legions of evil when they arrive from Hell. But she'll be ready food-wise.

I return to the concealing aisles of the store. I have a while. The picture on the box of frozen cherry blintzes has me salivating. I want one. The mouth is like a mini oven, and it will thaw there.

I hurry back to the frozen-food aisle and yank open the glass door. I had not noticed the boxes of blueberry blintzes next to the cherry. To their left are traditional cheese. I look for a variety pack, but the people at the blintz company haven't thought of that, or they have but would rather make us blintz enthusiasts buy three boxes instead of a single combo box. I will not be their dupe. I close the glass door, speed-walk back to the front of the store, and see Daphne exit with her bag of beer.

I am hungry, but I feel good. Hunger keeps you alert, to a point, after which it gives you a headache and makes you irritable. This is the good, motivating type of hunger. Animals hunt on empty stomachs, or why else would they bother. Which means it is hunger that compels the successful hunter. I'm glad I didn't get the blintzes.

I'm back in the car, ready to go, but Daphne is sitting in her car with the engine turned off. The large white bag from the vendor truck rests in her lap. She unscrews the cap from a bottle of beer, takes a swig, then unwraps a sandwich. As she chews, she stares into the night. I should have got the blintzes. Fuck.

I should stop thinking about food. Millions of years of evolution, maybe our keenest, most intense psychological drive is to crave. Crave food. Crave safety. Crave knowledge. Crave love. The gene for patience, however, remains low on the helix. We become educated, attain advanced degrees in science and the arts, create cities with startling technologies, we cure diseases, ride rocket ships to the moon, design robots that can transmit photos from Mars. Someone puts chocolate syrup in front of us, we drool.

Daphne finishes her sandwich, swigs down what remains in the bottle, then starts her car. She exits the parking lot onto River Boulevard, and a half mile later we merge with light traffic onto the 610 freeway going south. I hang fifty yards back. As we pass the interchange, I reach into the back seat for my baseball cap. If she checks her rearview mirror– new guy! I glance at my speedometer. We're doing eighty. Daphne is a speeder. Which makes sense, what with the adultery and the blackmail. I doubt she's wearing a seat belt.

There's a police car in my rearview mirror.

These guys are sneaky. They have the marked black-and-white Crown Royals with the big colored bars on the roof, but they're able to materialize out of the mist like a cloaked ship in a *Star Trek* movie. I slow to sixty-five and now drive with the caution and respect for the law of a newly elected mayor. My hands grip the steering wheel at ten and two and I stare forward, staying in the center of my lane, making sure not to tailgate. Which is what guys with six kilos of heroin in the trunk do. The police car pulls alongside. I look over amiably and nod, a sheepish half smile imparting: "Yes, Officer, I know I was speeding, briefly, but there's no heroin in the trunk." He nods, but minimally, imparting: "God has delivered you from a speeding ticket and higher insurance rates; I have been alerted to more urgent matters." He notes my gratitude and accelerates.

Daphne's car is a pinpoint in the hazy distance. Assuming that it's her. The Crown Royal takes the next exit, and I punch the accelerator. Eighty, eighty-five, still climbing. The pinpoint that might be Daphne veers right and shoots across three lanes without signaling. It's her.

I make the off ramp in time to see her taillights going left onto Decker Avenue. I follow a half block behind. I'm sitting up straight and have removed the baseball cap. Tall, short; cap, no cap: four permutations, four guys, but all with the same taste in cars. Daphne pulls into a drive-thru restaurant.

Ah, food at last. I whisper a solemn thank-you to God, then realize that after Daphne receives her new bag of food there won't be any time for me to get mine. I'll need to drive right past the food window. I tell God: You're very clever, aren't you.

I hear Daphne order a bacon cheeseburger, large fries, and four chocolate chip cookies. It's exactly what I would order. The voice in the box wants to know if she'd like a drink. She says no, but doesn't add that there are eleven beers on the passenger seat.

She drives forward; it's my turn. I must order something that doesn't require cooking. There are probably French fries ready to go, warm in a tray under hot lights. But then it hits me: cookies. I'll just drive up, give the woman some money, grab the cookies, and not wait for my change. I order four. I don't know how big they are, so I'll have to trust Daphne.

Daphne pays, is handed a bulging bag, and leaves. I hit the accelerator and screech to a stop at the food window, a five-dollar bill flapping at the end of my outstretched arm. But the woman has her back turned and is moving slowly. I can see she has the cookies and is reaching down, I assume for a bag to put them into.

"I don't need a bag," I say. "Just give me the cookies." I throw the five-dollar bill through the window.

This irks her, and she looks meaningfully at another employee who I cannot see.

"It's *fast* food," I remind her.

She looks at me, then back at the other employee.

"Shit," I say.

I leave without the cookies, and pass Daphne, who is parked by a wall. She has her cheeseburger in one hand, and a single French fry, poised thoughtfully before her mouth, in the other.

Experiences like this are evidence of God's existence.

I could drive around the block, reenter the drive-thru, and apologize to the woman at the window for my behavior, while she stares in disbelief at the other employee and demonstrates that no one, *no one*, is going to come in here and rush a fast-food worker and be rude and throw money at them and then, poof, expect a quick cookie.

Ten minutes later, Daphne tosses bag and beer bottle out the car window and we're off again.

We drive three blocks, and Daphne takes a right into the parking lot of Abe's Steakhouse. Maybe she hasn't eaten in days, would never have considered blackmail but she was starving. I drive past the restaurant and circle the block.

I enter Abe's Steakhouse. Daphne is sitting at the bar, eating Thai snacks out of a bowl. This is probably the meet. Boyfriend will arrive, see the envelope with all the money, they'll raise a glass. Or maybe Daphne will order a steak to-go and we'll hit the road.

I sit at a table in the corner, trying to get a waitress's attention. As several scurry past, my bladder sends a signal to my brain: I have to urinate. I don't really have to, but I'd like to very much.

A short, wiry man walks up behind Daphne and

sets his chin adoringly on her shoulder. She turns, sees his face, and shrieks with joy. They tongue kiss. Boyfriend has long, dark hair, slicked back with either some kind of gel or nature's version of it. He hasn't shaven in a while. He reminds me of those old prison movies in which the main character, who has been wrongly convicted, is befriended by a fellow inmate (Boyfriend) who promises to show him the ropes and take care of him, but eventually sells him to a rival gang for a carton of cigarettes.

My stomach tells my brain to put something in it and begins listing preferences. My bladder interrupts to say that it was not built to withstand the kind of unrelieved pressure it is now experiencing. But Daphne and Boyfriend could leave at any moment, so I ignore my straining bladder and stay put. A waitress arrives and sets a glass of water in front of me.

God exists.

I tell the waitress I'm starving, that I haven't eaten in eight hours, and I'd like a bacon cheeseburger with fries, then join my palms together, supplication-like, and request some pretzels, peanuts, Thai snacks, anything she can get her hands on right away. Daphne and Boyfriend stroll past. I tell the waitress never mind.

I follow the coconspirators as they are shown to a table, then double-time it to the restroom and urinate for so long that the man who enters the toilet stall as I begin is finished before I am. When I return, the coconspirators are studying their menus.

There is an empty booth across the aisle from them and, ignoring restaurant protocol, I sit there. I want to listen in. Maybe Daphne will address Boyfriend by his full name, I can call it a night.

Daphne examines each page of the extensive menu, then sets it down. Boyfriend is still on page one. Either he's a slow reader or he's checking for spelling errors. When the waitress arrives, Daphne orders a garden salad with fat-free dressing.

"Daph," says Boyfriend, "get some *food*, babe."

"Well..." says Daphne, re-eyeing the menu.

I am paying close attention to them, but using that trick where you hide your eyes by massaging the bridge of your nose as if you've got a headache or are trying to remember a phone number.

Daphne orders spaghetti and sausage with mushrooms. She hands the waitress her menu and glances in my direction. I continue massaging the bridge of my nose. She loses interest.

I notice a pair of knees and look up. A stocky young woman wearing a tuxedo-blouse is by my table. There is a well-dressed couple in their sixties standing behind her.

"Excuse me, sir, but did you give your name when you came in?" she asks.

"No," I say. "There was no one there."

"I'm sorry, this table is reserved. If you give me your name, I'll have you seated in five or ten minutes."

"Ah. Wonderful."

People have stopped eating and are staring at me. I slide out of the booth, my finger and thumb working the bridge of my nose. I am faint with hunger, tired and embarrassed, but the bridge of my nose feels great.

I return to the bar, where I can keep an eye on the front door and order a bacon cheeseburger with fries. Fifteen minutes later, I'm still waiting, but I don't pester the waitress. I am polite. I don't throw money at her and curse. When my food finally arrives, I want to shove the entire burger, followed by a handful of fries, into my mouth. But I eat slowly. I relish.

A young Irish woman is on a small stage playing guitar and singing about what she wants from a man. I listen carefully, but it's all very general– inspire her, make her feel special. I need details. After a half hour, Daphne and Boyfriend have still not left. At least not through the front door. I call the waitress over and ask if there is a rear exit through which someone might leave unobserved, an inappropriate question before one has paid one's check. I hand her a twenty and ask again. Yes, she informs me, there's an outdoor dining area in the rear with its own exit and, of course, another at the back of the kitchen.

It occurs to me that instead of tiptoeing back to the dining area to confirm that Daphne and Boyfriend are still here– which carries the risk of unwanted attention, even with the nose-bridge-massage tactic in full swing– I can simply stroll out to the parking lot and look for Daphne's car. This is called intelligence. I now see its value. Its application can really help a fellow out, reducing or eliminating risks and saving time. I will look into this with great interest when this whole fiasco is over.

Daphne's car is there. The restaurant door opens and here they come, Daphne laughing, a bag of takeout hanging from her elbow.

She and Boyfriend stop to kiss, caress. Finally, with a parting peck, they separate. After three steps towards their respective vehicles, they whirl on their heels and return to each other's arms for more kissing. They part, reunite, part, reunite. I am in my car, watching, waiting, sighing.

When they finally leave, in separate cars, I follow Boyfriend.

Daphne is behind me, and we proceed, slowly and evenly spaced, like a security detail. We take a right, and two houses down, Boyfriend pulls into the driveway of a decrepit house/shack with a post-apocalyptic lawn. I continue past, and watch my rearview mirror as Daphne pulls into the same driveway.

I have found the coconspirators' nest.

NINE

It is ten forty-five p.m. I circle the block, and park across the street from the coconspirators' nest. What now?

I mull it over, but it turns out I'm not good at mulling. Maybe music will help. It will relax my mind and winning strategies will flow. I slip a CD into the player, and Ben Webster's breathy, pitch-perfect tenor sax croons, calming me; thank you, Ben. Next, Led Zeppelin's "Stairway to Heaven," its mesmerizing intro guiding my spirit to a Zen-like place where focus comes easily; thank you, Zeppelin. Next up, the haunting pulse of the second movement of Beethoven's Seventh Symphony, which puts me to sleep; fuck you, Ludwig.

It is morning.

I have a vague memory of stirring at some point during the night, telling an orchestra to shut up, and clicking off the CD player. Also, I remember dreaming of cherry blintzes and Monica Zabrowski.

Monica sat next to me in second grade, and I wanted to marry her. In the dream, she had grown up but was still quiet and classy, and we were sitting next to each other in Mrs. Somerman's classroom, but in somewhat larger chairs. We were listening to Mrs. Somerman prattle on about multiplication and division while violently assaulting the blackboard with a piece of chalk. In front of Monica sat a plate of warm cherry blintzes. When she noticed me eyeing them, she said, "I sent you some blintzes. Check the mailbox."

I have not thought about Monica Zabrowski in twenty years. Before the next school year, she and her family had moved away. Then, in high school, she suddenly reappeared but was no longer quiet and classy; she had become, by my reckoning, just one more person whose main pursuit in life was to be popular. This saddened me, so I stopped thinking about her.

Sitting in my car, in the darkness, groggy and shivering, I spend a while wondering if Monica ever triumphed over the insecurity and consequent vanity that often accompanies adolescence. I take a pen from the glove compartment and write her name on the back of a fast-food receipt.

I replay the dream in my mind. Little Mrs. Somerman with the hair-trigger temper. The stimulating nearness of Monica. The plate of tantalizingly browned, buttery cherry blintzes. "I sent you some blintzes. Check the mailbox."

I get out of the car. Perhaps in that mailbox across the street is yesterday's mail with Boyfriend's name on it. I forgive Monica her straying from perfection, for she has emerged, magically, like a guiding angel, from the long-forgotten past to assist me during this spiritual trial.

I cross the street and stroll along the sidewalk towards the coconspirators' nest. My plan is to act disinterested in the mailbox on my first pass, venturing no more than a peripheral glance to see if its little door has been left open wide enough for me to see what's inside. As I approach, I am encouraged by the stick-on alphabetic letters on the side of the mailbox—perhaps Boyfriend's last name—but, upon closer inspection, I see they are only worn and tattered fragments, or Cyrillic.

The mailbox door is shut, and I continue past it to the end of the block before turning around. On the second pass, I will, in an apparent attempt to scratch my elbow, catch my finger on the mailbox door and open it, then continue walking. I will leave the peering inside and possible pilfering of United States mail for the third pass. I am growing increasingly nervous. When I arrive at the mailbox for the second pass, my finger flails in the air, neither scratching my elbow nor opening the mailbox. I'll have to do everything on the third pass. I discreetly scan the windows of nearby houses for observers, and the street for approaching cars. When I arrive at the mailbox, I casually open the door and reach in. There's a lot of mail. I grab it all.

"Hey, dickhead." A man's voice.

Two criminals– sometimes you just know– are walking angrily towards me. I could heave the bundle of mail at them and take off, but decide instead to play innocent and talk my way out of this.

The question now is, what credible explanation can one give when one is holding mail belonging to someone else at half past five in the morning? I must think fast, but what can I say? That I'm considering a career as a mailman and wanted to see what it's like? Not completely terrible, but no.

"What the fuck are you doing?" asks one of them.

They have me surrounded. One has a screwdriver dangling at his side, and it's not to fix the mailbox. The other is holding a baseball bat, and there's only three of us, so they're not looking for a game.

Screwdriver and Baseball Bat grasp my arms and lead me across the post-apocalyptic lawn and through the front door of the coconspirators' nest. The door closes behind me.

The lights are off, the curtains are drawn. Boyfriend steps forward. I hand him the mail. There is a bearded man in his forties sitting in a legless easy chair. He has an open book in his lap, but has paused in his reading to look up at me.

So, to help you follow along: we have me, Boyfriend, Baseball Bat, Screwdriver, and Beard. I don't know where Daphne is. I know *what* she's doing. Eating. But I don't know where.

"He's a cop," says Baseball Bat.

Boyfriend studies my face and demeanor. He's looking for telltale signs that say "cop."

"Why else would he be there all night?" asks Baseball Bat. His muscles twitch and flex with barely bridled violence. His tattooed physique suggests an indulgence in weightlifting usually associated with the freedom from petty demands, like a job, that prison allows. Hey, let's take the most vicious people in the world and make sure they have nothing to do for five or ten years other than joining gangs and lifting weights. Great plan.

"You a cop?" asks Boyfriend.

"No," I say.

He is skeptical. "Get his wallet."

Screwdriver takes my wallet from my back pocket and tosses it to Boyfriend, who flips it open. Beard has returned to his reading. I can see the cover. It is Jean-Paul Sartre's *Being and Nothingness.* He is halfway through, just getting to Nothingness.

Boyfriend leaves the room. No one offers me a seat, a cup of coffee, nothing.

"I read that," I tell Beard. "Sartre."

He looks up. *Being and Nothingness* is about self and the perception of self, and the perception of oneself as one perceives others perceive one, and the reemergence of valid self-perception after they've left the room or you stop giving a shit. Something like that.

"Enlightening, eh?" says Beard.

I nod knowingly. He returns to his reading.

A couple of minutes later, Boyfriend returns and says, "He's not a cop."

"Then he's a Fed," says Baseball Bat.

"You a Fed?" asks Boyfriend.

"No," I say.

"I gotta take a leak," says Screwdriver. He has been quiet thus far and now we know why.

"Go ahead," says Boyfriend. He puts a hand on the butt of the gun in his waistband so that I'll see it.

Screwdriver leaves.

"Why were you sitting out there all night?" asks Boyfriend.

Anything I say now, I'll have to stick with. Clearly, I can't tell him that I'm gathering information for Roger. That would open up new dimensions of hostility, maybe amp up the extortion demands.

"It's completely innocent," I say, and chuckle lightly. "I was driving and I got tired so I pulled over to take a nap."

"Bullshit," says Baseball Bat. "Why's he going through your mail?"

"Why were you going through my mail?" asks Boyfriend.

I sigh, like this is all so frustrating, but what I'm really doing is stalling. It's a terrific question. I blurt out the first remotely credible explanation I can think of.

"I was going to ask if I could use your phone, and I thought why not bring in the mail, you know, as a neighborly gesture?"

Boyfriend, Baseball Bat and Beard groan as one. They not only don't believe me, they think it's an incredibly bad lie. Screwdriver returns and looks around. He wants to know what all the groaning was about.

"Bullshit," says Boyfriend.

Beard smiles. He seems to appreciate the

difficulty of my position and the courageous determination with which I am confronting it.

Baseball Bat says, "You fucking…" and raises the bat.

"No," says Boyfriend, holding up a benign, imperial hand.

Baseball Bat lowers the baseball bat and says, "He knows, man."

"You trying to rip us off?" asks Boyfriend.

"What?" I say, acting stunned. "I just wanted to use your phone."

This time Screwdriver joins in the groaning, part of the team again.

"He knows about the coke," says Screwdriver.

The coke. Ex-convict comes into twenty thousand dollars, calls up ex-convict buddies. An order for a large amount of cocaine is placed, to be resold at a profit, a little bit skimmed off the top for personal use. And maybe I'm part of a crew who got wind of it. Unless I'm a cop. Unless I'm a Fed.

"Let me talk to him alone," says Beard.

TEN

With Baseball Bat trailing behind, I follow Beard down a hallway leading to the back of the house.

"This is bullshit," I say. "Can I at least use the bathroom?"

Beard gestures to a doorway on the left. I enter, but he keeps the door open a few inches in case I have ideas about escaping through the window by the toilet. I look around for something to use as a weapon, but there are only the normal bathroom items: a bar of soap, toothbrushes, toothpaste, a deodorant stick, toilet paper, a towel. The porcelain lid atop the toilet tank might be useful but would be difficult to hide under my shirt. I urinate and return to the hallway empty-handed. We march to the bedroom at the back of the house.

"Sit on the bed," says Beard.

I comply, and am approached by a dachshund who wants to smell me.

"Doris!" shouts Beard. "Get out!" He returns to the door, opens it, and Doris leaves, good natured but wobbling, as all dachshunds do, in apparent pain.

Beard has a gun, probably a .38, its barrel affixed with a tube that will mute the sound of fired bullets. Because bullets travel faster than the speed of sound, I alone, among those within earshot, would appreciate no benefit from the muting of a gunshot, unless, of course, I were to survive the gunshot, in which case the muting of it would seem paltry, as benefits go.

Baseball Bat stands with his back against the closed door. Beard brings a wooden chair over, places it in front of me, and sits.

"My friend would like a truthful explanation," he says, "of your presence here, last night and this morning, and of your interest in the contents of his mailbox, as well as the names of those persons with whom you are in cahoots, or who possess knowledge of your whereabouts."

"As your friend will remember," I say, matching his tone of gentlemanly formality, "he and I have discussed the matter, and there is nothing more I can add except to assure you of my truthfulness throughout the conversation in question."

"That is unfortunate," he says.

"Yes," I agree.

"Because it is my intention," he says, "to use any means I deem necessary to elicit the truth. However, it is not my desire to employ violent measures unless it appears there is no other avenue by which it might be acquired."

"First," I say, "let me commend you on your professional demeanor."

"Thank you."

"If one is going to be tortured, yea perhaps killed– and you may take it from one whose authority on the subject can no longer be rationally disputed– it is– and I must admit to being a bit surprised that it should matter at all– a *dang sight* better– to make use of a phrase favored by my paternal grandfather and which, by the way, I have never found occasion to use, but isn't it ironic that here, presumably at the end, I find its folksy patois somehow comforting–that it be a gentleman of erudition such as yourself performing said unpleasant task, rather than a goon of zero character, education, or sense of the profundity intrinsic to his task."

"It is rare that anyone notices," he says, "and unprecedented that it be expressed so articulately."

"You're very kind."

"Now," he says, "let us begin with the names of all persons with whom you are in league, or who possess knowledge of your present purpose and whereabouts."

"As I have tirelessly explained," I say, "there exist no such persons, since there is no ulterior purpose and therefore no need of persons to assist me in its realization."

"Fine," he says. "We'll come back to that. At this time, I would like to bring to your attention certain facts that may influence your impending decisions and, thusly, your future. First, the risks inherent to a stubborn reassertion of the aforementioned and, quite frankly, absurd explanation of your activities will by no means be borne by you alone. I will not hesitate to further punish any recalcitrance on your part— that is, after your nervous system has been rendered incapable of transmitting sensations of pain due to the overburdening and subsequent malfunction of its apparatuses—by submitting other members of your household– its location, of course, having been revealed by your driver's license– to a fate equally painful and crippling as your own."

"I live alone," I say. "I got a lady cleans the place once a week. You want to kill her, go ahead. She keeps moving shit around, I have to put it back."

He smiles, seems to be reaching back for something, I'm wondering for what, and the butt of his gun slams into my left cheekbone. The euphoric effects of my recent nap are completely nullified. Pain radiates through my head, discovers it needs more space and presses outwardly on my skull, which is unable to accommodate but tries.

"I'm afraid I must question your veracity," he says.

He reaches back again, this time I'm pretty sure for what, and the butt of his gun slams into my nose. The nose is extremely sensitive, there being a great number of nerve endings in the area, but the pain of a sharp blow can be minimized if you have recently suffered a similar one two inches to the left.

Baseball Bat chuckles.

My vision is blurred; it's probably the tears. I teeter on the bed's edge trying to look offended at having my veracity questioned.

Beard heaves a philosophical sigh.

"I'm afraid you leave me with no alternative," he says, "than to fire a bullet into one of your toes. This will, it is my hope, prevent you from again underestimating the consequences of persisting in games of evasion. Because if you were to do so– your name is Jacob?"

"Please. Jake."

"Because if you were to do so, Jake, then the painful and quite possibly deforming head injuries you have thus far incurred would merely be preliminary to a rearrangement of your body tissues, et al, on a much grander scale. I would have no choice but to insist that you remove your shoes and socks prior to my firing a bullet into the small toe of your right foot, after which I would continue across– one toe for each subsequent lie– until such time as you have feet but no toes." He pauses. His eyes say: Be reasonable. "Upon the eleventh lie– thirteenth if we include the two resulting in head injuries– I would proceed to fingers and thumbs. This would take us to twenty-two. Jake, living without toes and fingers would undoubtedly prove challenging, but you would still be able to carry out the majority of normal functions, such as standing, or applauding. If, however, you still persisted in the withholding of truth, the next to go would be your kneecaps. That would bring us to twenty-four. You would no longer be able to stand, however you would retain the ability to applaud, which is usually, though not always, done while sitting."

"That's true," I say.

"I'll admit to drawing a blank as to where we might proceed upon your twenty-fifth lie, but I'm open to suggestions."

"How about elbows?"

He thinks, nods. "That'd be it for applauding, though."

"Not necessarily," I say. "It just wouldn't be very robust."

"Good," he says. "That's twenty-six." He sits. "Now we arrive at the crucial moment. Will you continue to maintain that your appearance here is mere happenstance, that your interest in mail other than your own was a, quote-unquote, 'neighborly gesture,' and that there are no persons with whom you are colluding as regards your heretofore undisclosed and true motivations, or shall we finally acknowledge, en masse, that you have been a great deal less than forthcoming and that you wish to retain intact all joints and appendages, and, further, that the singular means to this end is to provide, forthwith, the information which, in my current capacity, I have been charged with acquiring?"

"I told you," I say, "I fell asleep in the car. I wanted to use the phone."

"Uh-huh. In that case," he says, "I trust you will understand that, given my position, I have no choice but to assume you are lying, and to proceed accordingly. I want you to know, Jake, that this assumption is not a product of any opinion regarding your fundamental character, having observed you during this brief yet revelatory interview, but rather of the inherent obstacles associated with my task, i.e., eliciting information from one who may be– and for entirely honorable reasons– obdurately disinclined to providing the names of persons to whom one feels a sense of loyalty and/or affection."

"Bravo."

About a year ago I purchased a self-defense manual, because I was too lazy and cheap to attend martial arts classes where students earn colored belts, enter tournaments, and bow a lot. This book was filled with sets of pictures, typically depicting a man or woman being confronted by an attacker in photo number one, and, by photo number five, standing over the fallen attacker, poised to deliver a devastating punch to his nose or throat. One section of this book dealt with defense against an attacker with a gun: gun from behind; gun from side; gun from front. None of the final pictures portrayed the would-be victim lying on the ground, bleeding from a bullet wound, relieved of wallet and valuables; the techniques seemed to work. According to this book, the first thing one should do when threatened with a gun is to redirect the gun's muzzle, via a swift sweeping motion of one arm, while simultaneously pivoting and backing into the attacker. The gun is then grabbed with both hands and given a sharp twist; if the attacker's finger is on the trigger, that finger will break. While the attacker is preoccupied with pain, one then executes a backward elbow strike to the jaw. Once the attacker has collapsed helplessly to the ground, one should kneel and strike either his nose or throat.

As Beard takes aim at the small toe of my right foot, I envision photo number one and proceed. I spring from the bed, swing my left forearm at the gun's muzzle, then pivot and back into him. I grab the gun with both hands, give it a sharp twist, and feel the resistance of his finger trapped within the trigger guard. Beard shrieks with pain and releases the gun. Baseball Bat (see *Six Weeks to Ultimate Combat and Self-Defense Techniques*, page 227: Multiple Attackers), has stepped forward and is raising his bat, but Beard now functions as my shield. I point the gun at Baseball Bat and fire at his chest. Beard, either having recovered from the acute finger pain or surging with adrenaline, grabs my wrist. I execute a backward elbow strike to his jaw, then follow with a single leg takedown that sends him sprawling to the floor. As he lies there, dazed, I kneel beside him, curl my raised right hand into a fist, pause for the photograph, and crush his nose.

Beard moans, his nostrils spurting blood, and looks up at me– not with anger but with wonder, as if he can't believe that I have prevailed with the timeworn gun-from-front technique.

I point the gun at him, and he perceives himself as I perceive him and I perceive myself as he perceives me and none of us want me to shoot him so he stays quiet. I listen for activity elsewhere in the house, but the shrieking and thumping and muted gunshot were probably assumed to be elements of the interrogation.

"All right!" I shout, feigning surrender before my tormentor to fool those who may be listening. "Stop! Please stop! I'll tell you!"

There is one more thing to do before opening the bedroom window and skedaddling. No, I will not kill Beard. He may be a sadist, but he's a bright one, and a seeker of truth. It's not that I like him. If I were to read in the newspaper next week that he'd been run over by a bus, I'd say, "Huh," and get on with my day. But I really am trying to become a better man, and while I'm fresh on this redemption kick it would feel wrong to kill *everyone* in the room. Not that I'm certain Baseball Bat is dead. He seemed like a tough guy who could take a bullet in the chest. I look over. All right, he's dead. I do have to knock Beard out, though. This will improve my chances of escape.

I position myself behind Beard, to spare him the dread-filled anticipation of knowing he's about to get hit on the head with the butt of a gun. But he turns his bloody head and watches me do it. He groans but remains conscious. I hit him again. Same result. I raise the gun a third time.

"All right, all right," he says, agreeing to be unconscious. He lays his head on the floor and closes his eyes.

I give his skull one last crack, then rush to the window.

ELEVEN

The coconspirators' backyard, as you may have guessed, looks like a monsoon has just swept through. Pieces of rotting furniture, scraps of ancient litter and empty beer bottles lay scattered among weeds. A twisted hammock is suspended at one end by the trunk of a gnarled tree, its other end on the ground perhaps in anticipation of a sapling that has yet to sprout. There is a wooden fence at the back of the yard. I hoist myself over into a neighbor's yard.

I contemplate my options. Should I return to my car? Or will Boyfriend and Screwdriver quickly discover my absence and arrive ahead of me? It's too risky, so I hop another fence into another yard. I hear growling.

The Rottweiler is an intimidating animal, and two of them are four times as intimidating as one. It's exponential. I turn, and find myself face to faces with two Rottweilers. I know a little about vicious animals, though. The most important thing is to not show fear. I begin acting like I'm in my own backyard with Rottweilers whom I saved, when they were cute little puppies, from a kill shelter. The Rottweilers aren't buying it. They keep growling, baring their teeth, that whole thing.

"How you doing?" I say cheerfully, as if they are no more imposing than mewing kittens. But these Rottweilers are not stupid; a little attitude is not going to throw them. "Want to hear a joke?" I say. "My girlfriend is a Siamese twin. And I'm seeing her sister on the side. Whoa! Hey!" I throw my head back and chortle. The growling stops and they watch me with diminished primal hatred. "Did you hear about the sixteenth century explorer who got eaten by cannibals?" I ask. "Talk about being consumed by your work. Whoa! Hey!"

One of the Rottweilers looks at the other one like: this guy's pathetic, I can't attack him.

Their interest in me is waning. I chuckle lightheartedly and stroll to the rear fence. I figure I have about four seconds before they realize that, yes, he *is* pathetic, *and* mildly amusing, but what is he doing in master's backyard? I leap up, plant my palms on the fence top, and hoist myself over into the next yard.

I follow a narrow pathway that runs along the side of this house, ducking under windows, then pass through a wooden gate that leads to the driveway in the front. There, I linger with palpable calm, untying then retying my shoelaces, so that if anyone happens to be watching I won't look like a sneak. I have no idea where I am, but I do have all my fingers and toes, and that's plenty to be happy about. We rarely know how good we have it. When something bad happens, we think how happy we would have been at that very moment if it hadn't happened. Which is bullshit. If it hadn't happened, we'd be griping about something else. Too often, we are petty and pessimistic. It's a cliché, but we rarely appreciate what we have until it's gone. But as I crouch in that driveway, untying and retying my shoes, I am in a state of ecstasy because I still have my fingers and toes. Lot of wisdom there.

What I must do now is find someone who will let me use their phone, so that I can call Tess. Boyfriend has my driver's license; her address is on it.

Bear in mind that I have just taken a severe beating to the face. There are welts and swelling and blood. Oh, yes, and pain. Which manifests in its own way: glazed eyes and a general aura of wooziness. I have to keep wiping the dripping blood from my nose with the bottom of my shirt, which adds to the mix a blood-stained shirt. Ding-dong. "May I use your phone?" "Why, yes, of course. Spot of tea?" It's six-thirty in the morning and not only would people be horrified to find me standing on their doorstep, they'd be irritated about having had to climb out of bed to do it.

I walk a few blocks; nothing but houses. I need an open business and a good lie to tell a proprietor or clerk that will elicit sympathy— and I don't have much time, because Boyfriend and Screwdriver may already be on their way to see Tess. After a good twenty minutes of futile trekking, I pause by a tree to think. A couple of squirrels are racing around and around its trunk in a rodent mating ritual. I watch three or four cars drive past, all headed in the same direction. They take a right three blocks up. It's a good bet they're headed away from residential and toward business, so I follow, and just around that corner is an open convenience store.

I enter. The clerk looks over and turns pale. He seems on the verge of announcing that he has several small children so please don't kill him.

"I've been in an accident," I say. "I need to use your phone."

He pauses to study my injuries as if I'm a triage pop quiz, then reaches into his pocket and hands me his cell phone. I thank him, put a little distance between us, and dial Tess.

"Hello?" she says.

"It's me."

"What do you *want*?"

"I have to see you. It's urgent."

She sighs the sigh I know so well. "I have to go to work in half an hour," she says.

"Trust me, Tess, this can't wait."

"Oh, my God," she says. "What's wrong with you?"

"I don't blame you for being upset, but I need to see you. And by the way, I've changed."

"You've changed." She chuckles.

"I'm growing up. I've stopped being an idiot who thinks there are no consequences to his actions. So believe me when I say this is serious."

"What happened?"

"I got in trouble with some drug dealers. They might be on their way to your house."

Tess supervises the tech department of a computer store, and in the ensuing silence I imagine her as a computer whose circuitry has been overloaded, freezing her. She reboots.

"What were you doing with drug dealers?" she asks.

"It doesn't matter," I say. "I wasn't buying drugs. There was a misunderstanding."

"Oh, my God. Call the police."

"I have to keep them out of it."

She reboots, sighs the sigh.

"Where should we meet?"

TWELVE

Tess is a short woman. She's from the Philippines, and therefore has black hair and black eyes and lots of weather. She looks like a cute Asian doll, but one that is five times smarter than you. I've never seen her look tired. Never. It's abnormal. If Einstein had met her, he would have acknowledged that sometimes E is a little more than MC squared. She sleeps, but it's like an electrical appliance that has been shut off. She is concentrated woman.

And now I have to lie to her, so this makes me nervous. But I know what to do: blame Roger. She'll believe that.

She arrives in her perpetually just-washed car. As I climb in, I observe her scowl. Tess speaks a lot with her eyes– people who look into them for any length of time seem to next spend a moment digesting what they have been told. With these eyes, she is about to begin a silent and scathing tirade, until she notices my battered face.

"What *happened*?"

"I'm fine." We are parked in front of the convenience store, the BMW's engine idling. "It was Roger. He got mixed up with some drug dealers and I tried to help."

"Oh," she says, her mood softening. Roger. Of course.

"He asked me to go with him somewhere," I say, "didn't say where or why. Before I knew it, I was jumping out a window and drug dealers were chasing me with baseball bats and screwdrivers."

"Oh, my God."

"They took my wallet, with my driver's license, and I was afraid they'd go to the house looking for me."

"Oh, Jake…"

She digs into her purse for her cell phone. "We have to call the police."

"We can't. Roger…"

"Screw Roger," she says. "I don't care about Roger."

I place a hand over the phone. "Tess..."

She looks up. Those beautiful eyes— eyes that once said: I love you, though much of it is based on your potential, not on who you are right now.

I must tell her the truth.

Tess is the only person in the world who I know beyond all doubt is good. I must confess what I've done. If anything were to happen to her, if Boyfriend, Screwdriver and Beard were to find her, harm her...

So I spill.

I tell her about the phone call from Roger, about agreeing to dump a hooker in the river, and taking money to do it. I tell her about discovering Louise's body inside the rolled-up carpet (she recoils and gasps and is still beautiful), and how I turned the tables on Roger and hid the body.

"Good," she says softly.

I tell her about the scheme to follow Daphne and

learn who her accomplice is, about how Daphne never stops eating for more than a half hour; about the house/shack with the dead lawn, and getting caught stealing Boyfriend's mail, about Beard and the gun—everything, including how grateful we should be for simple things, like having fingers and toes. She steals a brief glance at her fingers, and hopes I didn't notice.

We sit quietly.

After a minute or two, she puts the gearshift into drive.

"First we should get your car," she says.

"We can't. They might have it staked out."

"We can outrun them," she says.

"It's too dangerous."

"Jake," she says, "we have to take charge. We can't let the drug dealers dictate tempo."

"I know, but I want you somewhere safe. I can handle it."

We stare at each other, the memories burbling up from the depths of our own private sea of love. I know it's stupid and sentimental. But that's what it's like.

Her eyes say: From what I gather, you are lucky to have gotten away from these drug dealers, assuming we allow for the kind of luck that leaves one looking as if they've been pounded on like tenderized veal cutlet.

My eyes say: I appreciate the humorous veal cutlet simile, especially under such stressful circumstances.

"I got the guy's gun," I say, and lift my blood-stained shirt, revealing the pistol tucked into my waistband.

"Is it loaded?" she asks.

"Yes."

"Where's the house?"

I had not intended to return to the coconspirators' nest, at least not today, but two minutes later, here I am, rounding the corner onto what I now learn is Shenandoah Avenue. Great song, terrible street. It's a decrepit shantytown of cracked sidewalks and brown lawns, and smells like baked dog shit. "Oh Shenandoah, I long to hear you, away, I'm bound away..." A song that stirs up a longing for the pristine beauty of one's long-ago home. Someone had better start singing, and fast.

"Do you see anyone?" I ask, as we drive by my parked SUV. I am slouched down.

Tess glances casually around at the windows of the coconspirators' nest and other posts from which Screwdriver or Boyfriend might be awaiting my return.

"No," she says.

We go to the end of the block and turn around.

"What about the parked cars?" I ask.

"No one." She slows the BMW and says, "Now."

I open the door and roll onto the street, concealed by the BMW, while Tess pretends to search for something in the glove compartment. I insert the key into the door of my car.

"Jake," she says. "The front door just opened."

Staying low, I slide across to the driver's seat, slip the key into the ignition, and start the engine.

"Go!" I shout, and kick the BMW's door closed.

As we race for freedom, I check the rearview mirror and see Screwdriver run to the middle of the street, shout "Hey!" and give me the finger. He runs back to the house.

We haul ass.

Tess will go directly to work, where she will phone her neighbors and ask that they keep an eye on her house because she thought she saw a suspicious person lurking about. We will meet at my motel tonight.

In the meantime, I will talk to Roger.

So where am I now, I ponder as I drive, in this supposed new phase of life? If I'm to be honest, I still have a long way to go before I have become the man I know I can be. I must take responsibility for my wayward past, while avoiding further waywardness. I must set honorable goals and finish what I start, not get lazy and start taking shortcuts, et cetera, et cetera.

But principles are tricky: honesty can be cruel; sacrifice can be vain; courage can be reckless. For two days, I have labored to combine my new principles into a wisdom-filled, hierarchical glob of such intricate and profound structure that it will guide me in avoiding such pitfalls. Periodically, I have sensed the glob inside me shifting, settling, re-shifting.

And yet, for all my efforts, I have placed Tess in danger. My hierarchical glob has betrayed me.

THIRTEEN

I call Roger's home phone. I'm assuming that he's playing the role of distraught husband and has called his boss and done some method-acting and was told don't worry about work for a while, let us know if there's anything we can do, after which he failed to completely stifle a sob and said thanks and tried to hang up the phone but with all that method-acting grief he missed the cradle and it clattered to the floor but he was able to hang up properly after two more tries.

"Hey, buddy," he says.

"Got the name and address," I say.

"Outstanding. Let me get a pen. Okay, shoot."

I am silent. My hierarchical glob is spasming.

"Go ahead, buddy," he says.

My glob settles, then informs me that there remains no morally justifiable option other than to go to the police, confess all, accept my punishment, and stop assisting murderers. My glob reminds me that if I provide Roger with Boyfriend's address, there's a good chance Roger will have some nefarious associate kill everyone at the shack/house.

"Jake?"

"Forget it, Roger," I say. "My advice is that you get as much money together as you can, get on a plane, and go somewhere the police can't find you."

"Give me the goddamn name."

"What about Chile? No extradition treaty." I

made that up.

"I'm not going to fucking Chile." There is a long pause, then he says, "Jake, I never wiped your fingerprints off the credit cards."

"Bullshit. I saw you."

"Faked it."

"I gave them to you. Both our prints are on them."

"Not if I had pieces of Scotch tape on my fingers."

I unfurl a list of expletives and offensive terms. My hierarchical glob is snapping its fingers, trying to get my attention, it has instructions, but I tell it to shut up or I'll pass it out my ass into a toilet.

"Listen," says Roger, "you know goddamn well my alibi is airtight. But you were here that morning. Somebody could have seen your car, who knows? I could leave the credit cards where the police will find them and tell them Louise said she was having an affair with you and she was trying to end it but she was scared of what you might do and I told her she was crazy because you've always been a decent guy except for that time you killed those ants with the hose and that other time you pulled those snails out of their shells."

"I was eight."

"That's when it starts."

I seethe.

"Give me the fucking address," he says.

"I'll call you back." I hang up.

I manage a collection office. The lawyers are upstairs and we sue deadbeats, but first I get on the phone and see if they can't come up with eight hundred and fifty dollars instead of the fourteen hundred they owe and we'll call it even. I'm polite, unlike most in this business, so deadbeats love me and will pay me and screw everyone else they owe because I treat them well and make bad jokes and they're sick of collectors who threaten them and question their character, manhood and patriotism. They pay me, as if by doing so they're casting a vote for humanity. When my branch office is doing well, the people at corporate don't care if I take a three-hour lunch or sit around the office watching a baseball game or, to be honest, show up at all. We're having a good month, so I call and tell Tricia the receptionist that I might be delayed, which is code for: let me know if anyone with a say in my continued employment tries to get ahold of me and unless that happens don't expect to see me for a while.

Tess will arrive at the motel in a few hours, and I'm excited. It's the same excitement I felt when I was sixteen and on my way to pick up a girl for what would be my first real date. When I got there, she invited me in and introduced me to her mother and little sister (mom was divorced, so no dad to meet), and we all sat on the floor and played Monopoly, and the girl later confided to me that her mother told her I was special and not to let me get away. Which surprised me. I tried to figure out what made her mom say that. Maybe I'm being overly humble, but I think it just speaks poorly of other men. Tess looked at me today, just for an instant, the same way that sixteen-year-old girl did—like maybe she didn't want me to get away.

And what has been the catalyst for this miraculous renaissance? A criminal conspiracy. I helped a loathsome, subhuman schmuck evade justice for the most unforgivable of all crimes.

The irony is that it has turned out to be a good choice. It has marked the end of one chapter and the beginning of another. How can I regret entering into this criminal conspiracy when having done so may bring Tess back to me? Yes, I repented, I saw the light, I made a new start during the course of this criminal activity, but that might never have happened had I not gotten involved in the first place. Am I supposed to ignore the fact that Roger got the ball rolling by murdering Louise? Of course not. Let's say you're in a car accident that lands you in the hospital. While recuperating, you are attended to by an intelligent, sensitive, beautiful and lonely nurse. The two of you fall in love, marry and produce children who grow up to accomplish magnificent things in the fields of science and the arts. Do you now go around extolling the virtues of reckless driving because it precipitated marital bliss, monumental scientific breakthroughs, and awe-inspiring artistic masterpieces? No. But you *do* extol the idea that *whatever* happens, however awful, you should make the most of it. Because you never know– good things can come from anywhere.

At half past seven, there's a knock on the door. I let Tess in. She looks around.

"You live *here*?" she says.

I give her the tour: six steps to the bathroom and back.

"Let's go to the house," she says. "You have a gun."

I shake my head. "We can't be rash," I say. "Let's stay here tonight and think this through."

She sighs acquiescence and goes to the writing desk and sits in the creaky wicker chair.

"You hungry?" I ask. "We can have something delivered."

"You're gaining weight."

"I know."

"In your face."

I nod my head, but gently, to keep the flab on my cheeks from jiggling.

"Tess, I'm sorry."

"You should be sorry. It was wrong to sleep with the maid."

"I know."

"It made her uncomfortable. She left the country."

"When you said you wanted a divorce," I say, "I got very depressed. I didn't care about anything."

"You should have considered her feelings."

"I know."

She is staring at me now. I don't turn away, I don't change the subject. Her black eyes soften, as they once did by the glow of moonlight through the bedroom window.

"Let's go to a restaurant," she says.

I want to say "I love you." But I don't need to consult my hierarchical glob to know it's either too soon or too late.

FOURTEEN

Tess and I enjoy a quiet dinner at an Italian restaurant, neither of us broaching the subject of our marital situation. California law states that a husband and wife must wait six months, from the time papers are served, until a divorce may be granted. Human beings are highly emotional and rash by nature, so this is wise. But there are other reasons for a delay. A husband, for instance, considered by his wife to be a "lazy, selfish child," has six months to shape up and transform himself into a reliable, mature and thoughtful adult. If it takes longer than this, he has failed at lazy.

I must convince Tess that I am maturing, so I order baked fish. She pretends not to be impressed but I know her; she is. When the waiter asks if we'd like dessert, I don't ask for a chocolate sundae with chocolate syrup and lots of cherries on top. I order tiramisu, even though I have no idea what it is. It sounds sophisticated. Afterwards, I tell the waiter it's the best tiramisu I've ever had. He informs us that it is imported from Italy. I smile and nod knowingly; that explains it.

Back at the motel, Tess asks me to check what's on TV while she spends time in the bathroom getting ready for bed. I make myself comfortable on the floor with a pillow and bedsheet. When she returns and crawls into bed, I am not watching Spider-Man or Super Friends; I am watching a British sleeping aid called Masterpiece Theatre. There is no discernable plot to this show and every character in it is a full-blown archetype of someone I would try to avoid. For my money, it is no masterpiece, and just barely theatre, but Tess loves it. She watches with the intensity that I reserve for movies about cops trying to find out where the bad guys put the bomb. Eleven years later, when the show ends, we say our good nights, and Tess closes her eyes.

But I lie awake, thinking.

My first priority is protecting Tess, which means neutralizing the situation with Daphne and Boyfriend and their drug-dealing cohorts. Secondly, I must get ahold of Louise's credit cards, which supposedly contain my fingerprints. Thirdly, I must prevent Roger from finding out where Daphne and Boyfriend live and sending over assassins. Fourthly, I must avoid becoming entangled in the investigation of Louise's murder and the subsequent body-dumping should Roger be arrested. I fall asleep looking for fifthly.

In the morning, Tess calls the computer store where she works and tells them she'll be in late. She doesn't mention that drug dealers are after her husband and he can't go to the police because his fingerprints are on the credit cards of a recently murdered woman. She tells them her car broke down. Tess has never lied about such a thing in her life, so not only does her manager believe her but he decides on the spot never to buy a BMW.

Since she must stay away from the house for a day or two, Tess must do some shopping. Before she leaves, we have a brief strategy session. She's good at that, too.

I take a brisk walk to a coffee shop and order scrambled egg whites, wheat toast, dry, and orange juice; no pancakes, no greasy hashed browns. My God. Who am I? I recognize the face, but I can't place the food.

I return to the motel and call Clyde. Clyde is one of the collectors I supervise. He stands four foot six, weighs a buck twenty, but over the phone he sounds like a man who wrestles bears in the Yukon. He has a gravelly voice and gruff manner, and when he speaks to debtors on the phone, they are convinced that if they fail to make arrangements for monthly payments he will appear at their house on horseback, the bridle clenched in his teeth, and a double-barreled shotgun in either hand.

This, however, is not his greatest talent. What he is most adept at is locating people who have ceased contact with collection agents– or as we say in the business, "skipped out" on their debts. He is a master skip tracer.

Debtors generally fall into one of four groups. Group one is the honest folks, the salt of the earth fallen on hard times. They acknowledge their obligation and make arrangements, however meager, to resume payments. I call group two the "do what you gotta do" people. They are annoyingly passive.

They listen patiently as the collector explains their fiscal responsibilities and the potential legal consequences of noncooperation, and then say, in one form or another but always with exasperating calmness: "Well, you gotta do what you gotta do." I call group three the DNA's. This is not to suggest that they are genetically programmed to run up debt and never pay it back. It stands for Did Not Answer, "DNA" being the acronym left in their file notes several times each day, documenting that they have ceased answering the phone. Group four are the skips. They are the pros.

Being a deadbeat is a game to them. Sometimes they move to a new city without notifying the U.S. Postal Service. Sometimes they answer the phone and claim that they are not them but heard they moved to Buffalo. It is the debtor's version of hide-and-seek, and Clyde is one of the best seekers on the planet.

So I call Clyde and tell him I need the phone number corresponding to the address of the coconspirators' nest. Four minutes later he calls back with the number.

I dial.

"Hello?" says Daphne.

"Daphne, it's the guy who was at your house yesterday. I shot your friend."

"Hold on." She lowers the phone and I hear her say, "It's the guy who killed Kyle."

The phone is snatched from her hand.

"Hey, asshole," says Boyfriend.

"Hey."

He breathes quietly for a while, and I sense him staring into the pit of Hell, summoning the wherewithal to inflict sufficient torment to satisfy his wrath.

"How's it hangin'?" I ask.

More breathing. My casual tone has thrown him, possibly severed his connection to Hell's pit. My expectation is that this will further enrage him, but it is vital that he perceive no fear on my part. I await confirmation of his heightened rage.

"Fuck you!" Bingo.

"Hey, sorry about your friend," I say, "but he was about to hit me in the head with a baseball bat."

"You're dead, ass cunt."

I figure "ass cunt" is the worst thing a man can be called. I try to think of something more emasculating, but I can't.

"I'm not an ass cunt," I say, more to restore my sense of masculinity than to advance the conversation.

"Fuck you," he says. He has not reasserted that I am an ass cunt, so we're good.

"Guess what?" I say. "I'm a private investigator."

Silence.

"That's right," I say. "I was hired by Roger Kaplan."

More silence. Boyfriend is not a whiz at assimilating new information. Any conversation with him involving lots of new data takes on a Latin rhythm: Talk, talk, pause (cha, cha, cha); talk, talk, pause (cha, cha, cha).

"Don't know him," says Boyfriend.

"Well, he knows you. Said you were friends from a while back, and he paid me two grand to find you. I wasn't supposed to talk to you because he wanted it to be a surprise. That's why I was going through your mail— to confirm your name. Then I get the shit beat out of me and end up shooting a guy. Here's what I think. I think he knew about your little drug deal and wanted me to get your address so he could rip you off. Kaplan's a douchebag. He lied to me and I got screwed. Nobody fucks with me and walks away. So listen. I've got a way to take this asshole for a hundred grand and you're in if you want. Call me at my office if you're interested."

I give him the phone number of Velasco Investigations, where Tony Velasco and his associates have been instructed by Tony's cousin Tess to vouch for my employment as a private investigator if anyone asks. I hang up as Boyfriend is cha, cha, cha-ing.

There is no longer any reason for him to send Screwdriver and Beard to Tess's house to beat the shit out of me. Tess is safe.

FIFTEEN: THINKING OF TESS

I have had four romantic relationships. The first was Karen. I sat behind her in high school typing class and charmed her by drawing back the legs of her chair with my feet during the sixty-second typing drills. She would have to lean increasingly forward to reach the keyboard as the drill proceeded. At first, she found this delightful and hilarious. When she stopped laughing, I stopped doing it. Women will let you know.

The second was Leslie, who was introduced to me by Rosie, a wannabe matchmaker who worked at a Mexican restaurant I frequented. Leslie was from Colombia and understood about twelve words of English. As for me, I'd taken two years of largely forgotten high school Spanish, so our conversations were limited in scope and often confusing. Marriage seemed a possibility. She enrolled in an English-as-a-second-language course at a community college and promised to watch a lot of American television. It seemed only a matter of time before we would become a sophisticatedly loquacious pair of lovers. However, when I balked at marrying her immediately, she dropped out of language class, stopped watching American television, and forgot six of the twelve words she had known when I met her. If I would not marry her immediately, she communicated with no difficulty whatsoever, all bets were off. Women will let you know.

Number three was Jenny, who was living in the U.S. on a work permit. She had six months to find a husband or she'd be sent home to the Philippines. This was not explained to me at the outset. I had developed strong feelings for her when, one balmy night in late August, I was informed of the September marriage deadline. Marry her or good-bye. I didn't like how she'd handled the situation. I felt deceived. Women should let you know.

And then there was Tess.

I met Tess at a party hosted by a mutual friend. She was the smallest person in the room, but she has a denseness of spirit, and light is drawn to her and trapped there, like a black hole but in a good way. I asked for her number. Now, apparently there is a custom in the Philippines– I'm assuming there's a custom because this is what happened– that when a woman meets a man whom she wishes to see socially, she will bring a friend along on the first few dates. Tess does so, and the three of us go out to dinner. I pay for everyone, and I'm wondering if that's the purpose of the custom. After a few group dates, her friend ceases tagging along, and it's just us. We go to movies, to dinner, we take long walks on the pier by moonlight. I fall in love. We marry.

The sheer perfection of her makes each waking moment a dream, every slumbering dream a prophetic vision fulfilled upon awaking. If I search for a flaw, I am confounded. "Like a lily among thorns, so is my darling among the daughters." ("Song of Songs,"

Bible.)

Tess, however, is a mite less enraptured than the two beloveds of the "Song of Songs." My cheeks may indeed be as a bed of spices, but there's plenty of room for criticism elsewhere. I see perfection; she sees potential.

Then one day she announces: "We're too different."

The world grows dark and cold. I had it all; now I still have plenty, but it's pain and self-loathing and despair. I hate being unattached and find myself reminiscing about old girlfriends. Maybe there's hope with one of them.

I call Karen. She's married with two kids. I don't call Leslie. My Spanish has lapsed and we wouldn't get beyond hello, how are you, I'm fine. I don't call Jenny, she's either married or back in the Philippines.

Though we are divorcing, Tess and I still live together. She has the bedroom; I'm in the living room, which has a television and is nearer to the kitchen. Not bad. Lawyers are consulted. Papers are served.

One day the housekeeper, who comes on Thursdays, is dusting. She is aware that the living room is now my bedroom and we get to talking and I explain the situation. She is kind and consoling, which I need. The next week she returns and we hit the couch like a sack of randy lead. Afterwards, she gets back to dusting. When Tess arrives home for lunch, she takes one look at the housekeeper, who all but confesses to everything via a bout of sweating and stammering, and suggests that I move to a motel.

Now we are both at the motel.

SIXTEEN

My cell phone rings. It's Tony Velasco. He says there's a man named Bobby who's trying to reach me. Bobby is Boyfriend. Tony told him I was in the field, on a case. I grab my camera, go to my car and sit in the driver's seat. I open the windows to let in the sounds of the outdoors: birds chirping and cawing, vehicles rumbling by, the distant honking of horns. I dial Bobby.

"It's me," I say.

"I'm listening."

"Just a minute," I say, and lift my hands, in the shape of binoculars, to my eyes. "I'm tailing a guy whose wife thinks he may be cheating."

Bobby waits.

"Oh, my God," I say. "Let me get a picture of this."

I set down the imaginary binoculars and pick up the real camera. I aim, and click-click-click a series of photos featuring a lecherous shrub.

"Got it," I say. "They've gone back inside." I loudly scribble gibberish on a notepad, which takes a while because I'm very detail-oriented. "Bobby, I don't want to talk about this on the phone. Can we meet?"

"Where?"

I tell him where and remind him to bring my wallet.

Bobby is waiting in a booth in the bowling alley

diner. A bowling alley is a good place to discuss a criminal conspiracy, what with the balls rumbling, plopping into gutters, striking pins, then rumbling back through the underground tubes, and the people cheering and grunting and groaning. No one more than ten feet away can follow anything you say.

Bobby is enjoying a beer and staring at the lone waitress, who is at the other end of the diner taking an order. He is paying particular attention to her legs and thereabouts. I get his attention by dropping a stuffed manila envelope onto the table.

"This is for what happened to your friend," I say. "I'm sorry about that, but he came at me with a bat; it was him or me. It's ten thousand dollars. Split it with your friends any way you want. But this is nothing compared to what we can take that douchebag for."

Bobby stares at the envelope as if it's the legs and thereabouts of a waitress.

"Did you bring my wallet?" I ask.

He produces my wallet from his coat pocket and puts it on the table. I slide into the booth across from him.

"I haven't given Roger your address," I say, "and I'm not going to. My guess is he's planning to send a crew over to your house to take the money and the drugs. I'm stalling him, but we have to move fast."

"Okay," he says. "I'm interested.

Bobby may be humoring me. He has a perfectly good extortion of his own going, with the pictures Daphne took of Roger sitting on Louise's stomach and pushing a pillow into her face, but he likes the ten thousand dollars I just gave him. The more important inducement is that this way I won't provide Roger with his address.

"Listen, Bobby, I have no problem with how you make a living," I say. "But I prefer a simpler way. It's called blackmail." I lean back and smile as if I am enjoying awakening him to a whole new panorama of criminal possibilities. "Let me give you an example. The guy I was following today, I have lots of pictures of him with his little girlfriend, who happens, by the way, to be his wife's cousin. You think I'm gonna write that in my report and collect a lousy two grand?" I immediately regret the use of the word "lousy." If Bobby wasn't so stupid he might realize that I'm putting on an act inspired by movies from the forties starring Humphrey Bogart. "Hell, no. Tomorrow I go to the husband and tell him I don't approve of what he's doing—his wife is such a sweet girl and all— then sit back and wait for him to make me an offer." I smile. "No risk." I lean forward and lower my voice. "This guy, Roger Kaplan, did you know his wife just died? Insurance money's on the way. He can afford a lousy..." I silently curse myself, "paltry hundred grand if the alternative is getting arrested with a kilo of cocaine." I sit back and wait for the cheering.

Bobby is comparing his two hundred thousand dollar extortion scheme with my one hundred thousand dollar one, minus the cost of renting a kilo, minus my share. He looks at the manila envelope and decides they're both good.

"The thing is," I say, "he can't know I'm involved. I'll put the cocaine in his car, but you make the phone call and collect the money. Tell him the police will get an anonymous tip about a kilo of cocaine at his house if he doesn't pay."

"All right," says Bobby, "I'm in."

"One more thing," I say. "I want to talk to your friend, the one with the beard."

"Not a problem."

Bobby leaves and I bowl a game.

No offense to bowling enthusiasts – I don't wish to alienate or cast aspersions – but bowling has got to be the dumbest sport ever created. In golf, every hole is different: yardage, twisting fairways, trees, water, sand traps, sloping greens. In other sports the variables and permutations are endless. With bowling, it's the same damn thing every time.

To be fair, the arrangement of the remaining pins on a spare attempt will vary. Big deal. It's still a time loop. I'm guessing that the allure is that evasive perfect game. I lose this on the first ball. I start over. Lose it again. But all around me, children are laughing; I see the pride in people's faces when they bowl a strike. I feel an inner peace, induced by bowling's hypnotic rumbling, plopping, crashing, step-step-step-release simplicity. I bowl another game. I'm hooked.

Beard's name, it turns out, is Alan. I return to the

motel and give him a call.

"Yes?" he says.

"Alan, it's Jake."

There is a surprised yet respectful pause, if I may be allowed to read into a pause. "Ah, yes. How are you, Jake?"

"I'm well. I wanted to speak with you and make sure there are no feelings of antipathy between us. I have instructed Bobby to pass on a sum of money that, it is my hope, will serve as compensation for the pain and discomfort I have caused. He and I are in the midst of a new enterprise that will make the person responsible for that needless confrontation regret his reckless actions and be sorry he didn't think twice about them."

"Spare me the tautology. You and I are good, brother."

"Excellent. And the gentleman with the screwdriver?"

"He and I will speak."

"Alan, I must admit that I am somewhat astonished to be exchanging pleasantries with one who has so recently pistol-whipped me."

"'He who binds to himself a joy,'" says Alan, "does the winged life destroy.'"

"Ah. Yes." No idea.

When Tess pulls into the parking lot of Abe's Steakhouse at seven p.m., I am standing out front; I'm not sitting at a table inside already eating. I open the car door for her and do the same at the restaurant's entrance. I present her with a red rose as she enters. There is a confused look in her eyes, a hesitancy in her manner, as if she'd like to check my driver's license to verify that I'm me. I've opened doors for her before, I wasn't a total slouch, and I've given her flowers, but there was always the sense about it one gets when observing a dog walking upright or a chimpanzee playing a harp. I'm genuinely charming now.

We are greeted by the hostess that had expelled me from the reserved table while I was tailing Daphne. She remembers me, which I know because she frowns, which hostesses are trained not to do.

"Do you have a reservation, sir?" she asks.

"Yes," I say. "Of course I do." I give her my name.

She leads us to our table, her unenthusiastic manner conveying that I am not as special as the other customers. She is able, in subtle ways honed over many months of hostessing, to treat Tess as a valued guest without it bleeding over onto me.

"Tess," I say after the hostess has departed, having gently placed Tess's menu before her and thrown mine at me like a blackjack dealer with giant cards, "I have good news."

"Really?" She smiles. "What?"

"You can go home. I took care of it."

"How?"

"I talked to the drug dealers and gave them ten thousand dollars. Roger's money. We're all friends now."

I had never seen her looking so impressed. She is looking at me as if I have just liberated India from oppressive British rule by fasting.

"I'm sorry about all this," I say. "You know I'd do anything for you, right? That I would die for you?"

Tess and the waitress are speechless; both stare at me adoringly. I'm not sure how long the waitress has been standing there.

"Hello," I say.

"I can come back," she says, unable to completely suppress a tiny sob.

"No, that's fine. We'll start with coffee."

"Coming right up," she says, then smiles at Tess and leaves.

Tess and I are staring into each other's eyes, holding hands across the table.

"I'm not hungry," I say. "Let's go."

I leave a ten dollar bill on the table. The waitress will know what's up. As we pass the hostess on the way out, I tell her our table is now available.

We drive separately to the motel. When we get there, we are out of our cars and into each other's arms in four seconds. Our lips join like pieces of a jigsaw puzzle that lock together two halves of a picture of us. We haven't held each other in an eternity, so there's a lot of time to make up for.

"Jake..." she says, breaking away. "No."

She does that sometimes. She'll say "no" softly but sternly, like I'm a dog that forgot he was a dog and took a seat on the couch.

"It's too soon," she says.

I'm disappointed, but, still, I know these are the most wonderful words I've ever heard— "too soon" implies that its time will come. We linger within the aura of repressed emotions ready to burst forth, within the aura of a dead marriage suddenly resurrected, within the aura of intense glandular activity.

"All right," I say. We walk to her car and I open the door. "Good night, Tess."

Her eyes say: Soon.

I watch her drive away.

SEVENTEEN

Phase one of our plan was designed to protect Tess from the drug dealers who seemed likely to turn up at our house intent upon depriving me of fingers, toes, functioning kneecaps and elbows, and possibly life. If phase one proved unsuccessful, I had imagined, the drug dealers would show up at the house, encounter Tess, and demand she reveal where I might be found and crippled. She would refuse, of course, and I further imagined rushing to the hospital and finding a toeless, fingerless, et cetera Tess hooked up to a heart monitor, an I.V. bottle and an assortment of slings, a dozen doctors crowded around her trying to get a closer look because this one would get them published. But phase one worked. Onward to phase two.

The next morning, inconsiderately early, I drop by Roger's house unannounced. After ringing the doorbell, I stand to the side so he can't see me through the peephole.

"Who is it?" he calls.

I alter my voice and say, "Mr. Kaplan, please open the door," like a homicide detective with an arrest warrant.

He opens the door and sees it's me, but doesn't laugh giddily. He has slept badly. He is wearing a royal purple bathrobe over gold pajamas and looks like the emperor of a sleepy kingdom.

"What are you doing here?" he asks.

"We need to talk."

With the opposite of joyfulness, he nudges the door open and stands aside. I follow him to the kitchen table and we sit.

"What's going on with the police investigation?" I ask.

"They think it's a mugging."

"Are you sure?" I ask. "Because they always suspect the husband but tell him they think it was a mugging, and if he's stupid he believes it."

"What do you want?"

"A little voice in my head is telling me that if I give you the boyfriend's name and address you'll have him and Daphne killed. I can't do that."

"I *told* you, I'm not going to kill them." He raises his right hand as if swearing an oath, like otherwise I wouldn't believe him but his hand is in the air so okay. "I'm just going to *scare* them so they don't keep coming back for more."

"Bullshit."

He sighs. "Is that why you're here? To tell me that?"

"I also want to be sure you understand what you did. To Louise."

His face reddens with rage. He shudders with the effort of self-restraint. His bloodshot, sleep-encrusted eyes narrow, and convey a question: What the hell did you just say?

"I also want to be sure you understand what you did. To Louise."

"He sighs and rubs his eyes. "Let's not get into this."

"You murdered a terrific woman," I say.

"You smug piece of..."

"Shut up, ass cunt."

He is stunned. He has never heard this term before. He files it away for future use.

"You murdered a nice woman," I say.

"Go fuck yourself."

"'She should be alive, chatting with her friends, going jogging, reading a book, enjoying life; now, tomorrow, next week, ten fucking years from now. You robbed her of life and nothing can change that."

"You fucking. . ." his lips writhe; he seeks injurious words to spit in my direction, but he can't top ass cunt so he moves on. "She could have walked away, Jake, but she came after me. She wanted the house, alimony, everything. And she's telling everybody what a cheating asshole I am. She kept pushing. *She* chose this, Jake, not me."

"Okay," I say, "she wanted to punish you. Big deal. So you be a man and stand up to her. You didn't have to kill her."

He shakes his head like *I'm* the idiot sitting at the kitchen table.

"Let me ask you something," I say. "Did you *ever* love her?"

He scoffs. "Of course."

"I was thinking about the wedding," I say. "You and Louise walking around, both of you blushing. It was fucking adorable. I remembered a moment when you touched her shoulder lightly, as if she was delicate, and I was thinking, at the time, how this subhuman asshole I'd grown up with was learning how to be gentle. And you had this look on your face like you couldn't figure out why a beautiful, decent woman like Louise would marry you. Was that an act? Were you performing?"

His head droops; his bugged-out eyes seem at risk of falling onto the table, rolling off it, and plopping onto the floor.

"Get out," he whispers.

"She gave you a chance, and she was the only decent woman who ever will."

He looks like a dead body someone has propped up in a chair. I stand and look down at him with pity and contempt. When I leave, I close the front door softly; I don't want to interrupt his misery.

Roger keeps a spare key in a magnetized box concealed in the left-rear wheel well of his car. This is useful knowledge if you want to put a kilo of cocaine, provided by Bobby, in the trunk. As I do so, a flood of emotions surrounding recent events overtakes me—the hectic, stressful days spent aiding and abetting, spying, killing, worrying about Tess. It has been exhausting. I thought becoming a better man would be more pleasant.

I return to the motel and call Bobby.

He answers. "Dude."

"It's a go," I say, like we're NASA.

He will now call Roger and inform him that a kilo of cocaine has been planted somewhere on his property, and, as proof of his veracity, a silver dollar has been left inside an Audobon Society book on the coffee table in his living room but fail to mention it was me who put it there. Bobby will demand a hundred thousand dollars and assure Roger that unless he has a drug-sniffing dog handy he had better pay. If he doesn't, the police will receive a tip from a known gang member with an extensive rap sheet, now moonlighting as an informant, who will claim to have witnessed the drug transaction. Roger may well wonder aloud at this point why he is being extorted twice for two different amounts of money instead of once for their sum, but I have instructed Bobby to make the demand and immediately hang up sans further chitchat, which will leave Roger not only miserable but dumbfounded, too.

I spend the remainder of the morning reading, okay, also watching TV, and around noon call a Chinese restaurant to place a takeout order. I ask the man taking the order if they wouldn't mind stir-frying my sweet-and-sour chicken instead of deep-frying it. His manner changes abruptly, but I trudge on. I tell him that, while I know the lunch combo normally comes with egg roll, I'm trying to lose weight and if they put one in there I'll eat it, so could they please substitute a steamed dumpling or make the cabbage salad larger. He transmits, via an icy tone, his belief that I am one of those arrogant people who think everybody has to do what I tell them to do regardless of what's on the menu. He thinks I am an asshole. But not an ass cunt. I can live with that.

I drive to the restaurant and pick up the food, then return to the motel. The sweet-and-sour chicken has been prepared as instructed, however a giant egg roll stares mockingly up at me from its compartment in the Styrofoam container. I toss it in the toilet before I might succumb to temptation, but the toilet doesn't flush successfully and it continues to stare mockingly up at me as it floats, a little worse for wear. As I enjoy lunch, I watch *12 Angry Men*, starring Henry Fonda. It is a courtroom drama about the deliberations of a jury which deals not so much with guilt or innocence as with burden of proof. I watch carefully.

Afterwards, I call the computer store and ask for Tess.

"Hello?" she says.

"Hi."

"Oh, Jake." She sounds a little shy, as when we first dated.

"Did you sleep well?" I ask.

"*Very* well," she says, and laughs. After spending the night on the crappy bed at the motel, Tess was moving about stiffly for a half hour as if wearing an invisible body cast. She slept at home last night, and her mattress– our mattress– is two feet thick and would make the Queen of England feel guilty for living so well. It's like sleeping on a cloud.

"What about you?" she asks.

"I'm great. I called to ask you to keep a night open this weekend for dinner."

"Of course," she says.

"I'll call you later."

"Wait," she says. There's a pause. "How's... the situation?"

Ah, the situation. The murdered woman and my fingerprints on her stolen credit cards and my partnership with the drug dealers in an extortion scheme in which a kilo of cocaine has been hidden in the car of my ex-best friend who was the husband and guilty party in the case of the aforementioned murdered woman.

"Everything's aces," I say. "Nothing to worry about."

"Really?"

"It's pretty dicey."

"Be careful."

EIGHTEEN: BUNT

There is a game called sockball. It's like baseball except that, instead of hitting a small, hard ball with a bat, you hold a large inflated ball in one hand and smack it with your other fist. Otherwise, it's the same. Usually, one hits the ball as hard as one can, but sometimes, as in baseball, one taps it lightly and runs like hell. The defenders in the field, who were expecting the ball to come rocketing off your fist, are caught unawares, and by the time they realize they've been duped and have retrieved the ball a few feet from home plate, you are standing on first base having a good chuckle. This tactic, as you probably know, is called a bunt.

When I was in the first grade, the sockball-playing kids would gather at the start of recess and pick teams. As the two captains made alternating picks, the number of kids standing against the backstop waiting to be picked would dwindle until there was only one left, and one of the captains would have to choose him. On every schoolyard in the world, this last pick is, stereotypically, the kid with a drooling problem; the one who, if you toss him a ball, will thrust out his arms in a spasm of athletic futility while his knees buckle and the ball bounces off his nose or chest.

The two team captains were generally the best players, and the top picks were obviously the ones right behind them. These were the kids who could hit the ball really far. When they were up, outfielders were instructed by their captain to back up; no, farther; no, farther; no, keep going. I remember one kid named Jim who seemed to send the ball into Earth orbit. The next group, in terms of athletic ranking– numbers three through six of the nine on each team–would hit the ball over the infielders' heads, hoping to drop it in between outfielders. Picks seven and eight usually hit ground balls.

So I'm six years old and it's my first day on the sockball diamond and I'm watching the other kids. I see fly balls soar into the sky. I see others looped skillfully over the infielders' heads. I see weak grounders. Which type am I, I wonder. I don't know, because I've never socked a ball. I approach home plate, ball in hand. To conceal my insecurity, I take on a persona of caginess. I make a calculated accounting of the formation of the fielders, seeking holes in the defensive set, maybe a space between two outfielders where a ball might drop in for a double. Then, suddenly and without warning, I tap it lightly and run. I've got myself a single.

Next time, same thing.

For the next several weeks, I bunt every time. *Every* time. But these guys are no slouches, and soon the other team is sending fielders in to stand a few feet away from me as I go through the same drill: examining the outfield for vulnerabilities, calculating wind speed, what have you, before suddenly tapping the ball and running. A fielder, usually laughing, would pick up the ball and throw me out.

Having acquired this reputation, I am picked either last or next to last when teams are chosen. There was another kid who was sometimes picked last, which did create a little daily suspense, and a treasured, though hollow, victory for one of us.

The other boys started calling me "Bunt."

"Hey, Bunt." "Bunt is up!" It's Bunt! In! In! Closer!"

The reason I always bunted was simple: I didn't want anyone knowing what I was capable of. If I took my best swing at the ball, I would henceforth be defined, in my capacity as an athlete and sportsman, by the distance it traveled. Better not to know, I decided. Better to keep it a mystery. We could all wonder what would happen if I ever gave the ball a good smack.

One day Roger and I are riding our bikes, and we find a sockball. This is something of a miracle. You might find baseballs and tennis balls in the street, the occasional football or basketball. But never sockballs. They are strictly schoolyard stuff. Yet here, as if left by some mysterious benefactor, is a fully inflated sockball.

We take it to my house and we're tossing it around when Roger says, "Why do you always bunt?"

I shrug and say, "I like bunting," and shoot the sockball at the basketball hoop in my driveway so that we'll be playing basketball and not discussing why I always bunt.

"Why don't you hit the fucking thing?" he says, a six-year-old who says "fucking" blazing the trail for us stragglers. He tosses me the ball.

"Nah," I say, and take another shot at the basketball hoop.

He retrieves the ball and tosses it to me. "Take a swing," he says.

And I trust him. I know there's plenty wrong with him, but I know he won't laugh at me. I give the sockball a good smack. It travels high and far—third-pick distance.

The next day at recess I approach the batter's box. Three or four fielders gather around home plate. It's as if the game has stopped and we're having some kind of conference. Someone yells, "Hey, Bunt!" and laughs. And I send that goddamn ball flying over him, over all the infielders, even over the left fielder, who was expecting the usual amusing spectacle of my "surprise" bunt.

I was never picked last again. Because Roger said to hit the fucking thing.

That's Roger, too.

NINETEEN

I work out. I run in place, drop to the floor for push-ups, roll onto my back for leg lifts, then jump up and jog around the motel room, back and forth, back and forth; push-ups, leg lifts, jogging, again, again, again. Sweat dripping to the floor, I jog to the bathroom and get a towel. When that towel is drenched, I replace it with a fresh one. After panting comes huffing, then gasping, and I have to ease up to catch my breath. Night falls. I'm still going. Every muscle is burning, so I slow to a walk, pacing back and forth; pacing, turning, pacing, turning, like a panther in a cage. I finish with a stroll to the deli five blocks away and pick up a half pound of lean roast beef, a sliced bagel, some cucumber salad and a carton of orange juice.

After dinner and a shower, I stand in the bathroom looking in the mirror, and see traces of Teenage Jake beneath the retreating layers of jowl and cheek flab. Hello, Teenage Jake. Nice to see you. For a moment I'm in high school again, but feel stressed at the prospect of approaching midterms and quickly return to the present. There are new challenges and fears to confront here in the adult world, but are they really as daunting as a biology exam you've spent less than fifteen minutes studying for? I'm not sure.

I call Tess to tell her about my workout. She has just returned from the gym where she has completed ten miles on the treadmill, thirty minutes of core training, and a self-defense class with kicking and punching to music; she has stolen my thunder. We make plans to see a movie over the weekend, then say good night. There is a tender moment of silence. We say good night again.

In the morning, I am a giant sore. Walking is painful. Spreading jam on an English muffin is painful. My aching muscles, if they could talk, would be grumbling and drooling.

The plan we have devised calls for me to acquire the pictures of Roger murdering Louise that Daphne took with her cell phone. I must get this phone and forward the pictures to mine. Once I have them, I will inform Roger that if anything happens to me, if I am struck by lightning, or arrested for Louise's murder, or if my body is found behind a rock by a jogging trail in the foothills, my lawyer will send an envelope containing the incriminating pictures of him to the district attorney in lieu of a campaign donation.

I arrive at the coconspirators' nest at eight p.m. carrying two large pizzas, two six-packs of beer, and a bottle of tequila. I am greeted warmly; I, too, am a coconspirator now; their nest is my nest. Even Doris the dachshund is happy to see me, though we have met only once, and then for just a cursory sniff. Bobby, Daphne and I eat, drink, and toss slices of pepperoni at Doris.

Doris, due in part to the accuracy of my pepperoni tossing, grows fonder of me by the minute and soon falls asleep on my foot. I am charming when I want to be; Daphne and Bobby may soon be sleeping on my other foot. Shots of tequila are poured.

"Hey, man," slurs Daphne, "where'd you grow up?"

She and Bobby are splayed on the couch like frozen skydivers. They've had a lot more alcohol than I have because I've been dumping my shots of tequila onto the carpet before pretending to throw them back lustily. I want them drunk; I want them asleep. I launch into a fake story of my life that I hope will finish what the drinks have started. Then I will find Daphne's cell phone, send the pictures of Roger to mine, grab the last slice of pizza, and boogie.

I am gambling that neither of them has read *David Copperfield*, because his childhood is fresh in my mind. I was regularly beaten by my stepfather, I tell them, but received some measure of revenge when I bit his hand, after which he flew into a rage and gave me a thrashing. It turns out that Bobby also bit his father's hand. We bond. They are not getting sleepy.

I keep going. After exhausting young Master Copperfield's exploits, I am, by turns, Oliver Twist, Tom Sawyer, and Holden Caulfield. After a youth spent picking pockets and seeking treasure, I was sent to a psychiatric hospital. Daphne is so engrossed in my story that she has stopped eating; a slice of pizza rests, forgotten, on her thigh.

I pour more shots and move on to the Hardy Boys Mysteries. Daphne and Bobby are pleased to learn that I have a brother. Frank and I are pretty close, I tell them, and after my release from the mental hospital we opened a private detective agency. I recount the case of missing persons Chet and Biff that put us on the map. Now it's John Steinbeck's *Of Mice and Men.* Frank, I tell them, is a towering lummox who is always getting into trouble, so eventually the agency shut down and I found employment at Velasco Investigations.

"That's quite a life," says Daphne.

"Shit, yeah," says Bobby.

I pour more shots. Three minutes later they are unconscious.

I head for the bedroom at the back of the house. Daphne's purse is on the dresser and I dig inside; no cell phone. I search everywhere but can't find it. I get Daphne's keys out of her purse and sprint past the sleeping coconspirators on my way out to her car. I search the glove compartment, the trunk. It's not there. Next, the kitchen. I check inside the microwave oven. I am desperate.

I stand for a moment, sweating, panting. If only I could call her cell phone from mine, listen for its ring—but my only contact with either of them has been on the land line, the number Clyde at the agency acquired in four minutes. Cell phone numbers are much tougher to find. There wouldn't be time.

I have failed. I have fumbled the football on the one-yard line in the fourth quarter of the Super Bowl—God help Leon Lett— I have let a ground ball trickle through my legs in the bottom of the ninth inning of the World Series— God help Bill Buckner— I have called for a time-out when my team didn't have one in the NCAA Finals—this one is a little less self-explanatory but it probably cost Michigan a national championship— God help Chris Webber. While I am in good company—these were terrific players— I mustn't give up.

In times of trial, I like to think about those throughout history who have faced seemingly insurmountable obstacles, how they persevered in spite of powerful adversaries because they knew that their cause was right: Galileo, who stood by his belief that the Sun, not the Earth, was at the center of the planetary system; the Founding Fathers, who asserted that all men are created equal and endowed with inalienable rights; the time that Saint Louis Cardinals center fielder Curt Flood refused to be traded to the Philadelphia Phillies and, though the Supreme Court eventually ruled against him, initiated the long yet inexorable series of events that led to professional athletes making zillions of dollars.

There's a video of a speech made by college basketball coach Jim Valvano that I watch on my computer now and then. He was dying of cancer, and he stood in front of a big audience and made them laugh and cry and think. And his message was this: Don't give up. Don't ever give up.

I'm standing in the kitchen, refusing to give up. And the idea comes to me. Of course.

I dial Roger on my cell phone.

"What?" he says.

"Call Daphne."

"Why?"

Why, indeed. I can't tell him that I'm attending a pizza-and-booze get-together with the blackmailers and need to find Daphne's phone, or he's likely to connect me to the cocaine extortion plot.

"Bobby just walked in here with another woman," I say. "I'm at Abe's Steakhouse. They're all over each other."

"Who gives a shit?"

"This is our chance, Roger. Divide and conquer, right? Get Daphne down here right now."

I hang up and listen for the ring. I think I hear it, but no, Bobby is snoring. He sounds like a vibrating cell phone. The seconds tick by. Then, finally…

I hear it, the blessed sound, like heavenly chiming. It's coming from the back of the house, so I sprint past the coconspirators, down the hallway, and into the bedroom to find Doris in the final phases of a bowel movement. She steps back from her work and watches me nervously like a playwright awaiting reviews after a disastrous opening night.

The phone rings again, and I shut the door to keep its sound from reaching the front of the house. I whirl around. Doris seems braced for a harsh rebuke. I scan the room and wait for the next jingle.

When it comes, I leap onto the bed. The phone is beneath a bedsheet— of course I didn't look there;

who sleeps with their phone? I open it, then hang up. I take out my own phone and dial Roger.

"She's not answering," he says.

"They're leaving," I say. "Shit." I hang up.

In the bathroom, I take a seat on the toilet and open the photo folder in Daphne's phone. I scroll through the pictures: Daphne sporting a pair of Mickey Mouse ears at Disneyland; Bobby sporting a pair of Mickey Mouse ears at Disneyland; Doris sporting a pair of Mickey Mouse ears by the busted hammock in the backyard; Bobby raising a glass of beer in a bar, surrounded by a slew of laughing partyers; a slew of live lobsters piled on top of one another in a tank in a restaurant, none of them laughing.

In a weird way, pictures of Roger suffocating Louise would in no way seem incongruous.

I find the pictures, send them to my phone, delete my number from Daphne's list of outgoing calls, put her phone back in her bed, and tell Doris she can take a dump wherever and whenever she likes. I get the hell out of there.

TWENTY

The next morning I make an appearance at work. The predicted end-of-month numbers are good. My branch wins a lot of the "Best Branch Office" awards handed out by corporate, and there are more than a dozen plaques and trophies on the walls and shelves of my office. At annual get-togethers I am paraded around in front of the other managers like a favored child before his loser siblings.

After reviewing this month's numbers, I tune the radio to a classical station, lean back in my chair, and close my eyes to think. They're playing a slow movement from a Mozart piano concerto. It's gorgeous. According to the movie *Amadeus*, Mozart was murdered by a jealous motherfucker. The heinousness of this murder is compounded by the loss of the beautiful music he had yet to compose. I deplore murder, of course— those who are not sociopaths do— but I am obsessed with Louise's murder. And now Mozart's, as well. I turn off the music. It's making me angry. My hatred for Roger has become nearly unbearable. I want to kill the motherfucker. Hell, I want to kill all motherfuckers. There must be a lot of them. The newspapers will be reporting about the new serial killer in the area, the Motherfucker Killer. Motherfuckers everywhere will be locking their doors and windows at night and trembling in their beds wondering if they're next.

It's time to wrap this shit up. I call Roger's cell.

He answers. "What?"

"We have to meet."

"Why?"

"I have new information. It's the last time. Are you home?"

"Yeah." He hangs up.

He answers the door wearing pajamas and a bathrobe and holding a piece of toast. He hasn't shaved in a while. His eyes are not merely bloodshot; they are oval coagulations of blood that watch me coldly. I follow him to the kitchen and we sit at the table.

I take out my cell phone, open the photo folder, and set it on the table before Roger. I have selected a picture that shows him sitting on Louise's stomach and pressing a pillow against her mouth, really putting his weight into it. Her arms are outstretched, trying with her fingernails to slash at his face, which he keeps out of range by leaning back. He is wearing golf apparel—short pants, woolen sweater vest over polo shirt, and visor. You look at the picture and think: Why didn't he just hit her with a golf club?

Roger stares at the picture.

"I've sent copies," I tell him, "to my attorney in a sealed envelope. He knows he's not to open it unless something happens to me. There's a note in there with your name and the name of the detective handling the case and Daphne's name and address so she can tell what she saw."

Roger sets his toast down.

"I want the credit cards with my fingerprints on them," I say. "Then no one will ever see these."

"How did you get them?" he asks, his first words since my arrival.

"I stole Daphne's phone," I say. "And put it back. She never noticed."

The oval blood coagulations widen. "You had the phone?"

"Yes."

"Did you delete the pictures?"

"No." The reason I didn't, of course, is that Bobby and Daphne would have known it was me who did it.

The oval blood coagulations narrow. "You idiot!"

"They probably have copies."

"You don't *know* that!" He picks up the remaining corner of toast from his plate and heaves it at the cupboard.

"I'm not trying to help *you*, Roger," I say. "Only myself."

Roger drains the last of his coffee, then stares at the table. It is as if we are playing chess and I have announced checkmate and he is examining the board for an escape I hadn't noticed.

Finally, he pushes his chair back and stands.

"Wait here," he says. "I'll get dressed.

Ten minutes later we're in Roger's car gliding along the freeway by the rocky hills. Up ahead lies the jogging trail where we left Louise's body only a few days ago. Disregarding the cardinal rule that advises enlightened criminals to never return to the scene of the crime, this is what we are doing. It occurs to me, as I stick my head out the window to let the wind whip through my hair, that not only are we returning to the scene of the crime, but we're doing it with a kilo of cocaine in the trunk. Talk about pushing your luck. I look at Roger. He looks like somebody the police would pull over on a whim. I only let him drive because I know about the cocaine. If the car is searched and the cocaine is found, I can act shocked and deeply disappointed and all that.

We arrive at the jogging trail and park.

"Fuck," he says, looking around. There are several parked cars, though no people in sight.

"Stay here," he says.

The sky is overcast; there's a chill in the air. Good jogging weather. He gets out of the car and starts walking. A male jogger in gray sweats, red-faced and puffing, staggers through the opening between the high rock walls and steps onto the dirt parking lot. He stops, bends over, and places his hands on his knees. He will either spend a little time catching his breath or keel over and die.

Roger is not dressed for jogging—he wears slacks, a thick coat over a flannel shirt, and the kind of heavy-duty black shoes a plumber might favor. His general appearance suggests a looming need for an I.V., but he starts warming up. He raises his arms over his head and stretches side to side, then bends forward, working the hamstrings, trying to touch the plumber shoes. He jogs in place and rotates his head to get the neck loose.

The puffing man hobbles towards Roger and passes him on the way to his car. They exchange greetings, and Roger goes into a squat to stretch the thighs, then stands, swinging his arms forward and back. Finally the guy drives away, and Roger is ready for bed. Casting a nervous glance at the entrance to the trail, he walks to the edge of the lot where rests a pile of rocks. He removes the top layers, then digs something out buried at the bottom. He returns to the car carrying a folded towel.

He opens the door, tosses the folded towel at me, and gets in. I unfold it, and there they are: four credit cards belonging to the late Louise Kaplan. I use the towel to wipe away all trace of fingerprints.

We make the silent journey back to Roger's house.

When we arrive, I go to my car. But as I'm about to drive away, I stop. With the engine idling, I call Roger over.

He stands at the window of my car.

"Roger…" I say.

This is good-bye. Good-bye to decades of a once sure and steady friend; good-bye to a pal to watch football games with, to throw back beers with, to bitch to about the boss and the old lady and the president, to laugh with about stupid shit only we understand. My lifelong icon of buddy-ness.

"You look pathetic," I say.

He nods, and breathes a quiet, "Yeah."

"Always remember, Roger," I say, "this wasn't my doing. I thought we'd be friends when we were ninety-nine."

He sighs.

"I gotta survive, right?" I say.

He thinks, then says, "All right, buddy. It's on me."

We are quiet for a while, feeling time pass, sensing that a page of the book of life has turned to a new chapter.

"You may not believe this," I say, "but I wish you well."

I reach out my hand. He grabs it with surprising vigor. I don't know if that's a tear in his eye, but he has never looked so human, never so possessed of such a complex emotional makeup. I reach out my other hand so that both of mine surround his, then let go. I show him the credit card in my palm that now bears his fingerprints.

"You give me any trouble, the D.A.'s gonna have a case that'll put him in the conversation for governor."

I drive away.

EPILOGUE

A week later, Bobby called to tell me that Roger came through with a down payment and I should go get the kilo out of his trunk. I said hey, why don't I just keep the kilo in lieu of my share of the money, and he said yeah, why not. So one night, very late, I went and got the cocaine from Roger's car and threw it in a dumpster behind a liquor store where a few lucky rats would have the night of their lives.

Tess and I have started over. There was always love between us, but it just as often drove us crazy as sent us soaring. Now there's respect. And trust. And the feeling that we are becoming two halves of one person. It's a slow process. I'm still at the motel, but I don't sleep in my pants and shirt anymore. I do still eat in bed, but that's only because I'll be moving out soon so it doesn't matter if the mattress smells.

That's all I'm going to tell about - this is what the guy says at the end of *The Catcher in the Rye*, which I read in high school - that's all I'm going to tell about, just like him.

I find myself thinking about the profound questions of life more than I used to. Like: Where did we come from? And: Is God real? This last one seems so absurd: that there's - as I once heard it put - a man in the sky wearing a white robe and judging us. But maybe God wants it that way. Maybe he wants to see what we do when we think no one is watching.

ABOUT THE AUTHOR:

Steve Lerner attended the University of California at Santa Barbara and California State University, Northridge, and received a bachelor's degree in music composition, focusing on jazz. He is a contributor to Yellow Mama magazine. The Book of Jake is his first published novella.

Made in the USA
Las Vegas, NV
15 February 2021

17935383R00090